STICKY FINGERS

VOLUME 4

JT LAWRENCE

FIRE FINCH

ALSO BY JT LAWRENCE

FICTION

SCI-FI THRILLER
WHEN TOMORROW CALLS
• SERIES •

The Stepford Florist: A Novelette

The Sigma Surrogate

1. Why You Were Taken

2. How We Found You

3. What Have We Done

When Tomorrow Calls Box Set: Books 1 - 3

URBAN FANTASY

BLOOD MAGIC SERIES

1. The HighFire Crown

2. The Dream Drinker

3. The Witch Hunter

4. The Ember Isles

5. The Chaos Jar

6. The New Dawn Throne

STANDALONE NOVELS

The Memory of Water

Grey Magic

SHORT STORY COLLECTIONS

Sticky Fingers

Sticky Fingers 2

Sticky Fingers 3

Sticky Fingers 4

Sticky Fingers 5

Sticky Fingers: 36 Deliciously Twisted Short Stories: The Complete Box Set
Collection (Books 1 - 3)

NON-FICTION

The Underachieving Ovary

ABOUT THE AUTHOR

JT Lawrence is a USA Today bestselling author and playwright. She lives in Parkview, Johannesburg, in a house with a red front door.

∼

www.jt-lawrence.com
janita@pulpbooks.co.za

f facebook.com/JanitaTLawrence

🐦 twitter.com/pulpbooks

a amazon.com/author/jtlawrence

BB bookbub.com/profile/jt-lawrence

DEDICATION

This book is dedicated, with love and thanks,

to my Patreon supporters:

∾

Joni Mielke

Elize van Heerden

Nigel Perels

Claire Wickham

Wendy Durison

Sian Kitsune Steen

Megan Guzman

∾

Thank you also to my dedicated proofreaders,

Keith & Gill Thiele, and to all my loyal readers.

I wouldn't be able to do this without you!

STICKY FINGERS

VOLUME 4

CONTENTS

1

BRIGHTSIDE

The oat porridge that morning had been made without milk or sugar. The Wizard of BrightSide had warned us this day would come. It would be something to celebrate. It would mean it was time to leave the Orphan House for somewhere better; somewhere far away from the acid clouds and city smog of Akeratu that made us cough in the sooty playgrounds. There would be meadows, he said—I didn't know what meadows were—and clear skies and trees with green leaves and shade. He said there would be flowers in the fields like colourful buttons on a carpet.

We love buttons here. They are much-prized possessions. I couldn't imagine them just strewn carelessly on a carpet, no matter how green. You can use buttons for lots of different games; you can do magic tricks for the small children; you can trade them for sweets. I tried to picture flowers in a meadow. We were surrounded by cold grey concrete, hard metal chairs, and thin, dirty mattresses. The building stole the warmth from your blood and made your bones ache, so the idea of lying on soft grass in the sunshine made me long for it deep inside my body as I longed for my parents and Milla Mouse, my little sister.

Mouse had cheeks like those crisp pink apples we used to get before the bitter rain ate the blossoms. Before the silver drones and the explosions and the smoke.

I pushed the acrid-scented memories from my mind and forced my thoughts back to Milla; her apples for cheeks and naughty smile. Her belly laugh. Her small teeth were perfect, despite her habit of climbing on the kitchen counter and eating sugar out the dented silver bowl. She would have been three years old now.

Even the weeds there are pretty, the wizard had said once, his cheeks flushed and his eyes sparkling. *And you can blow their seeds—they look like feathers—you can blow them into the breeze and make a wish.*

But the Wizard of BrightSide wasn't always so cheerful.

The future is no place for children, he had said the week before. We were in his sparsely furnished office, looking out of the window at the ash falling from the sky like snow. Absentmindedly, he put his hand on the back of my neck, where my barcode was.

The past was better. The sky used to be blue, the most beautiful colour you've ever seen. And the grass was soft and green. 2054 is not a good year for children.

I didn't know what to think about that. I didn't know what the future was. All I knew was that I once had a home and a family I loved, and now they were gone. Because of this, I had a black emptiness in my stomach which never went away, even on good days. Even when there was plenty of milk and sugar, and the nurses would sneak us extra biscuits at tea time.

I knew things could be worse; I had heard the whispers. At least at the Orphan House I had a bed to sleep in and food to eat. And I had the wizard, whose tender palm was still resting on my neck. My eyes travelled down to the windowsill, and I saw the silver envelope there. It had the Sheng insignia on it, and the top of the paper was jagged where the envelope had been slit open.

His hand tensed on my neck, and my muscles stiffened along with it. I was never afraid of him; he was a kind and generous man, and if he had a temper we never had once witnessed it. He forbade the nurses to spank us or hurt us in any way. But I was scared of what he might say about the official-looking silver letter. I wanted to know what was inside, but I was also afraid.

I dragged my eyes from the envelope and gazed up at him. His face looked like one of those charcoal clouds that thundered in and threatened to pelt us with hot shocks and searing rain. He sighed, then forced an affectionate smile.

But things will get better, Kitsune, he said, and I nodded. I liked it when he said my name; it made me feel important. And I knew the line from the book. I knew every line in the book. *Things will get better,* it said on page 28, the one most smudged by small fingerprints. *They always do.*

The Wizard of BrightSide was not a *real* wizard, but we liked to call him that, and I think he liked it, too. He wasn't like a white-bearded man in a fairytale, but he was magical in his own way. Before he built the Orphan House, he had worked as a doctor in a children's hospital where he wrote books to cheer his young patients up. The nurses told us that his most popular book—*The Wizard of BrightSide,* where he got his nickname from—sold thousands of copies and that he was famous, even in some parts of Sheng, where he was born. He received a medal of some kind from the mayor in the Akeratu city hall days before the building was razed by the silver drone bombers. Akeratu is in the East, and Sheng is in the West. We don't have a wall to divide us but a greasy black river called the Fiume. They say it used to be clear water, sweet enough to drink, but now it runs with ash and blood. I don't know where the ash comes from.

The Wizard of BrightSide was a story about a poor boy who discovers he has supernatural powers and has to learn how to believe in himself and how to control his magic. At the end of the book, he saves the people he loves with a special magic trick. We'd all read the book; of course we had. We had a few copies to share but with almost two hundred of us—greedy for stories that would make us forget the nagging ghosts that spilt cold mist into our limbs—the pages were brittle and dog-eared, and the curved spines had been sewn and taped over and over.

My mom taught me to read when I was three. She was a journalist and author. We had a lot of books at home, so I know a lot of words, more than some grownups do, and I read stories to the tots. We call the one and two-year-olds the tots and it's our job to look after them. The nurses do, too, but there are only twelve of them and—as they like to remind us—they only have two hands. Not like the silver soldiers. But I don't like to think about that.

Orphan House is no ordinary orphanage. That's what the wizard says. He says we're all extraordinary, and that's why we wear our badge every day, to remind us that we're important. It's a pale blue diamond shaped piece of fabric the size of a copper crown. We wear them proudly over our hearts. The wizard doesn't wear one, and neither do the nurses. You can only wear a blue diamond if you're born on the East side of the Fiume, in Akeratu. The people born to the west of the black river don't wear badges, and they don't have barcodes on their necks. They speak Sheng—the same language as the silver soldiers—a language we don't understand. I feel bad for them sometimes. Wh can't they be special, like us? Especially the wizard, and the nurses. I thought it would be fairer to get a badge if you were a good person, instead of where you happened to be born. If the authorities knew what they were doing, they'd take Jakko's badge away for bullying the tots and give it to the wizard, instead. Jakko pinched the babies and stole their biscuits, which was really mean, because usually we were only allowed one cookie a day, at tea time. Sometimes the idea of that biscuit is what got you through the day.

The day we ran out of milk and sugar the sky was its usual shade—the colour of a dirty old facecloth frayed from too much boiling and wringing out—and it was raining. We weren't allowed to play in the rain. The acid would sting your skin, and the cold echoed in your skeleton for hours afterwards. There were no more antibiotics, and even the little white pills they used to give us for our fevers were running out. There wasn't enough wood to keep the heating stove burning all day. We used to have heaps of firewood; mountains of it. We'd hunt for branches and kindling in the forest, but we aren't allowed to go into the woods anymore.

The black emptiness in my stomach churned the whole day after eating that plain porridge because I knew things were going to change. I was looking forward to the better place; to the blue skies and clean air. But I also had a bad feeling, like the one I had when the Sheng soldiers came into our house and my mom told me to hide in the dog kennel. I hadn't wanted to leave her, hadn't wanted to squeeze into the little house that smelled of old dog breath, air abuzz with mosquitoes. Jumpy with nerves, I had begun to argue, but she hissed and shoved me away, tears in her wide eyes.

Remember the plan, her pale lips whispered. So I ran to the kennel and scraped my skin getting inside so that it was raw and bleeding.

Sometimes I wished that I'd stayed with Mom there at the kitchen table, then I wouldn't miss her so much, because I'd be dead, too.

Things will get better, said the Wizard of BrightSide. *Today we begin our adventure.*

He instructed us to dress in our finest clothes, our most comfortable shoes, and to take extra care with our morning routine of tooth-brushing, face-washing and hair-combing.

Even though I'm a boy, I'm good at doing the tots' ponytails and braids because I used to do Milla Mouse's hair. Jakko makes fun of me for this and for wearing my mom's locket around my neck.

Kitsune, Kitsune, he says. *Kitsune's a girl.*

I don't care. I don't see anything wrong with being a girl. My mom was a girl, and she was the best person I ever knew.

Get lost, I tell him. What I really want to say is *Go and get lost in the forest,* but that would be a terrible thing to say because everyone knows what happens to children who stray into the woods.

When we were all smartly dressed and had gargled with mint tea (mint grew like weeds all around the house, despite the snow ash and sour rain), we were told to pack a knapsack.

Only one change of clothes, the nurses said, *and your favourite toy. And don't forget your lucky buttons.*

That cheered me up. If we were only taking one outfit and one toy it surely meant that we would be getting new clothes and books and things to play with. Even my smartest outfit was faded and scruffy, and I was forever trimming loose threads from the seams with the rusty little pocketknife I found under the cracked floorboard in the dayroom. The navy blue blazer I was wearing was the smartest thing I owned, but it was a size too small. At fourteen years old I was one of the oldest orphans, so there were very few hand-me-downs. The idea of new, comfortable clothes lit a flame of hope inside me. The sound of the rain beating against the roof faded to a hiss and then to silence. Maybe the wizard was right, I thought, as I straightened my jacket. Maybe things would get better.

Knapsacks packed, faces shining, we were ready for our departure. The tots grasped their cuddle toys to their chests, their pale faces stamped with confusion. They wanted to know where we were going, but no one knew the answer. "The meadows" meant nothing to them, or us.

"Our new home," said Nurse 3, her expression stern. Nurse 3 was usually stern, so that didn't worry me too much.

We stood on the warped timber of the front verandah, spilling out down the broad steps that used to be grand but were now peeled back to splintering dry wood. The wizard had his backpack, as did the nurses. The nurse's bags were grey, matching their tunics, but they had left their aprons behind. The wizard took a breath and looked around at us, patting Salome's shoulder and mussing Frederic's hair. It was as if he was breathing in the energy he required for our adventure, even though the air burned your lungs if you drew it in too deeply. I guessed it was difficult to leave the house he had built, the memories he had helped create. Even when you know you're going to a better place, it can still feel sad to leave. The nurses looked upset, too, and wore gashes for lips instead of smiles as they herded us down into the front yard of wet sand and soot. At least it had stopped raining.

We heard the rumbling of heavy vehicles far in the distance. I had assumed we would have to walk to our new home in the meadows, but it looked like the wizard had arranged transport. It couldn't have been easy; any fuel was challenging to come by. I was relieved. My shoes were too tight for me, and I could already feel a blister beginning to swell on the back of my heel. I had imagined a trek through the evil forest, tripping over roots, fighting off monsters and carrying the tots when they were tired, so I was happy to hear the engines coming our way.

But when I saw the two trucks approach, splattering black slime and mud, my relief twisted into dread. They weren't school buses; they were cattle trucks armed with silver soldiers. The drivers wore no blue diamonds over their hearts. The robotic Sheng soldiers jumped out, their built-in radial rifles hidden by the shimmering uniform they wore that looked like silver water.

My immediate instinct was to run. I remembered my mother's protestations, and then her screams until the *rat-a-tat-tat* of the robot's weapons silenced her. I remembered the feeling that it could not be real, could not possibly be real, but the needle-bites of the mosquitoes —like pinching yourself in a dream— made me understand it was. I hadn't wanted to hide. I had wanted to save my mother, but the glint of the silver through the kitchen window paralysed me.

In a way, I was trapped in that moment forever, because in my mind there was no moving past such a heart-shattering thing. I would be squeezed in that musty kennel forever, skin scratched, bleeding and bitten, fright freezing me in place. I suppose a part of me did die with her that day.

Seeing the silver soldiers again filled my body with a fiery fear as if I would burn up right there on the flaking stairs. I could hear the mosquitoes in my ears. Why were they here? Were they not the enemy of Akeratu? Some were robots, some were human, and some were a mix of the two. They shunted the backs of the trucks open with a bang and barked in Sheng. I didn't understand the language, but their meaning was clear. We were to climb in and not waste their time. The nurses held the tots' hands and led them towards the growling vehicles, shushing them and comforting them as they did so. I wanted to run in the opposite direction, wanted to escape the shimmering water uniforms, but I knew I could not. I had been a coward before, frozen in the kennel, but this time I would be brave, like the boy in the book the wizard had written. Instead of running away, I picked up the crying toddler standing next to me and wiped her tears away with the back of my hand. It was Kiki, a sweet toddler I had a soft spot for because of her belly laugh. She reminded me of Mouse.

"It's okay," I said to Kiki, moving toward the giant groaning vehicle. "It's okay. You'll see. Things are going to get better for us. Today our adventure begins."

A little boy—Benjamin—refused to get into the truck, so Nurse 9 had to force him inside, and he began to scream and scream, despite the soldiers yelling at him to keep quiet. The roar of the engines drowned out his crying, and I was glad, because I was sure the men wouldn't hesitate to leave him there on the edge of the dark forest, ready to be snatched up by the horrors that lived therein. The dirty brown fabric flaps were down. We didn't get a last look at the Orphan House, so we were denied a final glance to say goodbye. It was hot and crowded, and we stood squashed together, a hundred children per truck. We took turns to sit when our legs gave way. The vehicle smelled of cow dung even though I hadn't seen a cow for years. They must still exist, I thought, or we wouldn't have milk for the babies or for our breakfast porridge.

The motion of the cattle truck and the stinky broth of exhaust fumes and excrement made my stomach swirl. I held onto Kiki—the tot I had picked up on in the front yard—and swayed and patted her, holding her tightly despite my nausea and wobbly legs. The nurses huddled amongst us, and when Benjamin's wailing became unbearable they began to sing, and we all joined in. We sang hymns and anthems and the theme songs to the television series and adverts we used to watch before the satellites went down. We sang every song we could think of and Ben stopped sobbing and fell sleep in Nurse 9's arms, his body slack and his head drooping like a spent flower over the woman's shoulder. We played games with our fingers and toes and our buttons. The nurses shared the food they had brought in their backpacks: stale bread, raisins, and some of the small sour oranges we were able to grow in our makeshift hothouse outside the girls' dormitories. There was not enough water for everyone to have a drink, so I told Nurse 4 that I was not thirsty.

The trip lasted for days that were squeezed into hours. Infinite minutes that rolled on and on like marbles down a slope. I lost all concept of time and didn't remember sitting down to sleep. When I woke up, Kiki was sitting next to me, singing a nursery rhyme as if it were an ordinary day.

Hours after I awoke, exhausted and slick with sweat, the trucks finally stopped. My bladder was so full it was cramping, which I had never felt before. Every time it cramped I squeezed the large yellow button I kept in my pocket. The button had been a gift from the wizard on my arrival at Orphan House, and I kept it with me at all times. It was my lucky charm; a promise that things would get better.

While my bladder sent spasm after spasm through me, the smaller children were not able to hold it, so it was a relief when the rough men finally banged the truck doors open, and the fresh wind whipped the reek of urine away. Nurse 3 demanded the soldiers give us water to drink, but the robots fingered their rifles and told her to stand back. I ran to the closest tree and relieved myself behind it, my cheeks alight with shame as I heard the soldiers laughing at me. Again I had the urge to run, and again I decided to stay.

I felt delirious with hunger and dehydration, and my legs felt strange and heavy on the solid ground after the continuous motion of the vehicle. The sun was too hot. I couldn't face getting into the cattle cars again for the next part of the journey, but I needn't have worried. The giant tyres kicked sand in our eyes as the trucks rumbled away, leaving us pale and blinking in the too-bright sun. The drivers left; the soldiers stayed.

I didn't understand. Where were the meadows, where was the soft grass and blue skies? I spotted the wizard's tall frame in the crowd, wanting to ask him questions, but he didn't see me. He was too busy tending to the orphans who were weak with distress. All around us was a wasteland. *Even the weeds there are pretty,* the wizard had said. But, looking around, I saw that even the weeds were dead.

"Congratulations, children," the wizard said, straightening up so that we could all see and hear him. I noticed the strain on his face, and his smile was pulled down at the edges. "You all did an excellent job. Now, the hardest part is over, and we have only good things to look forward to."

The atmosphere lightened a little, but I was put off by the smirks I saw on the soldiers' faces, and for the first time I understood that this trip had never been the wizard's idea. We were standing there, ill and hot and shivering, because of that silver envelope on the windowsill. The official Sheng letter had been an instruction, not an invitation.

"We will now march," said the wizard. "Just as we have practised." That meant smartly, with our arms at our sides and our chests proudly displaying our blue diamonds.

Still disorientated and disillusioned, we lined up in our marching rows, like sick little sergeants. The nurses flanked us, and the wizard took his usual position at the front. The older children marched at the back. It was our job to make sure that no child was left behind.

The wizard gave the signal, and we began to march along the path lined with dead shrubs and saplings. There was an odd smell in the air, and the human soldiers put on their masks, which were monstrous contraptions; the things nightmares are made of. They were replete with night-vision visors and a pipe snaking to their mouths: a bullet-proof oxygen delivery system.

We marched and marched and marched, the smell getting stronger. Our adrenaline pushed us forward. When children fell or fainted, we picked them up and carried them. Nurse 8 managed to carry a baby in a sling on her chest as well as a tot on her back. I put my shoulder under Salome's when she began weeping from exhaustion, and we hobbled along. My blisters burned my heels like hot coals. Kiki fell. I had to let Salome go so that I could pick her up. Despite my exhaustion, her body felt light. Her lips were white and dry. We kept marching.

Finally, a huge wrought iron arch announced the name of our destination. It was a scary looking sign, like one would find at the entrance to a graveyard instead of a fancy new town, or a meadow.

"Finally!" said the wizard. "We made it."

We all looked at him, half-delirious from the struggle. The sign was in Sheng, so we couldn't read it. He took off his hat and wiped the sweat from his forehead and neck, then put it back on his head.

"Welcome to BrightSide," he said.

If that was what a meadow looked like, I thought to myself, then it was sorely disappointing. On the outskirts, the landscape was arid, and the horizon beyond bristled with dead trees. There were people strewing ash in the fields, perhaps as fertiliser, but nothing was growing there. In front of us were squat concrete buildings. The tallest one was dome-shaped, cracked and speckled with smoke—a grey boiled egg—and there was nothing before us that looked remotely more attractive or hopeful than the Orphan House.

I could no longer see the soldiers' expressions beneath their masks, but I was certain they were smirking again. I tried to put the puzzle together in my head: the silver drones, the silver envelope, the shimmering silver soldiers who had gunned down my mother—an enemy of the Sheng state—in cold blood, leaving her lying in a bright puddle on our kitchen floor. The same floor we had swept white flour from after baking, the same tiles that Milla had crawled on when she was a baby, then taken her first unsteady steps. The kitchen floor that was now grouted with black blood, if it existed at all.

We walked under the black-lettered archway and were soon at the largest of the ugly buildings. The one behind it belched the foul reek that permeated everything; a tall chimney that reached into the grey sky, constantly spewing the evil-smelling smoke. I almost stumbled, but recovered just in time to not drop Kiki. We streamed into a large courtyard which looked so bright and bleak at the same time that it overwhelmed the smaller children and they began to cry again.

"It's all right," assured the wizard. "It's all right. You've all done so well. I am proud of you."

Kiki was still in my arms, unconscious, her hair plastered to her forehead with perspiration, reminding me of Mouse after her afternoon naps. My arms were starting to shake. My muscles needed a rest, but I couldn't put Kiki down. I didn't want to put her down. The stink was terrible, and the grey snow fell on our shoulders and hair.

· · ·

There was a human soldier stationed at the entrance of the building. He was in Sheng military fatigues—not the shimmering uniform—I guessed he didn't need to be invisible here. The man shouted a command at us in Sheng, but I didn't understand. The size of the automatic rifle that hung from his shoulder conveyed all we needed to know. He switched to our home language, Ake. "Remove your clothes!" he yelled.

The orphans looked around, wondering if they had misheard. Were they all going to get new clothes now? I remembered dreaming of the new, comfortable clothes that morning, but I could see by the nurses' expressions that there were no new clothes here. They were trying to hide their fear, but I could see it in their eyes. Slowly, reluctantly, they began to help the smallest children undress.

The wizard removed his hat again, approaching the man, proudly but with humility. I slowly crept to the front of the crowd of children, staying on the sidelines. I wanted to hear what they were saying as they talked in hushed voices.

"Let them wear their clothes," the wizard said. "Please."

At first, the soldier in fatigues who had just barked at us looked angry, but then his face changed into one of recognition, then surprise. "Hey," he said, speaking Ake, his eyes lighting up. "You're that famous doctor."

"Yes," said the wizard.

"You saved my brother's life," he said. "At the Children's Hospital in Saja. You're the author of my favourite book."

"I'm glad about your brother," the wizard said. The soldier seemed shocked at seeing the wizard, then his body relaxed, losing the sharp angles of aggression.

"Would you like a cigarette?" He opened a dented silver case and offered it to the wizard. It reminded me of the sugar bowl we used to have at home.

No," said the wizard, shaking his head. The soldier took out a hand-
olled cigarette for himself and snapped the box shut.

Let's go for drinks tonight." The soldier tapped the cigarette on the
op of the case, then put it to his lips and lit it. "There's a place at the
»arracks that serves decent vodka. The food is edible ... if you've got a
trong constitution."

[he nurses had tears streaming down their cheeks, but they kept their
aces as neutral as possible, not wanting to upset the children. I
.ssumed, looking at the soldier's chafed rifle, that crying children got
hot.

I'm going in with the children," said the wizard.

[he soldier looked like he had just been slapped. His mouth hung
»pen, the cigarette sticking to his bottom lip. "You're what?"

I'm going in with the children."

What?" exclaimed the man. "They're Akeratan!"

Could you keep your voice down?" asked the wizard. "I don't want
hem to be scared."

They're orphans!"

They're my children," the wizard said.

But ..." the man struck his own temple. "You were born Sheng! You
on't need to go in there. You're crazy!"

[he wizard gestured at the soldier to keep his voice down. He shook
.is head, his eyes rolling skyward; he couldn't believe what he was
earing. His eyes darted up at the nurses and then back to the wizard.
[e tried one more time, in a low tone. "There's a back door inside the
hamber. I'll unlock it for you now. You can go inside with them and
hen leave quietly while they are not looking. No one will ever know.
Ve'll be drinking vodka tonight. I'll buy you dinner."

"Thank you," said the wizard.

The soldier looked relieved. "So you'll meet me at the back?"

"No. I'll stay with the children."

I could see the soldier's jaw muscles working, chewing on his frus tration.

The wizard persisted. "Now, will you allow them to keep their clothe on?"

The soldier's face hardened into a grimace. "It's a lot of extra work fo us." I thought he was going to say no, but in the end, he dragged on hi cigarette and nodded. "Fine." He looked at his watch and then tippe his head to indicate the open maw of the building. Tobacco smok leaked out of his mouth. "But you'd better move it. The next grou] will be here soon."

The nurses were weeping openly now as they shepherded the chil dren through the doorway, shored up by the silver soldiers. The nurse didn't have blue diamonds on their chests or barcodes on the necks, s I don't think they were allowed in. The wizard seemed to be the onl exception, because he was famous and important. Nurse 8 took th baby she had been carrying in the sling on her perspiration-staine chest and passed him to the wizard, whose hands I saw tremble.

As the wizard led us through the door, the barcode detector in th doorframe counted us one after the other: beep, beep, beep.

There was nothing to look at; just a large room with some dull met; piping on the walls, like a communal shower. Were we supposed t shower? I wondered if that's why the soldier wanted us to take ou clothes off. The floor was painted a toxic-looking green. Kiki was sti. unconscious, and I was glad. I didn't want her to be afraid. Benjami attached himself to my right leg and didn't let go. The door slamme shut, and the seal was activated. My eyes met the wizard's. He gave me a fond look; not quite a smile. I nodded at him as if we had an understanding, because it felt as if we did, even if I hadn't yet fully grasped the consequences.

Things will get better, Kitsune, I imagined him saying to me, his hand tenderly holding the barcode on the back of my neck. *They always do.*

It was hot with all of us crowded in the room like that, and the air was thick. The babies began to cry, and then scream, which scared the tots, who started wailing, too. I saw Jakko pick up a tot and hold him tight, swaying him, comforting him. I grasped my mother's locket and kissed it.

"It's going to be okay," said the Wizard of BrightSide, grasping a child's hand. He was holding the baby in one arm. There were some dull banging noises from outside of the room, and then a hissing sound in the walls. He spoke loudly. "I want you to all take your lucky buttons out."

The children did as instructed. I shifted Kiki's weight to my left hip so that I could access my frayed blazer pocket. My hands were shaking, but the sight of the bright yellow button made me feel better. The children nodded at the wizard, clutching their buttons, eyes shining with tears.

"Now," he said, his voice calm and strong. "I have a secret to tell you."

The whispering and wailing tapered off as we listened to what he had to say.

"I am, in fact, a *real* wizard," he said. "And I'm going to show you my best magic trick."

I bit my lip, watching him, holding onto Kiki while clutching my yellow button, Benjamin still glued to my leg. A strange chemical smell filled the chamber.

"Now ... hold on to those buttons as tightly as you can and think of the best place you can imagine in the world. If you wish hard enough, your lucky button will become a portal, and you'll be magically transported to your own BrightSide."

I thought of the pretty weeds the wizard had told me about, how you can blow the little seed feathers away into the breeze and make a wish. I looked down at my yellow button, then squeezed my fingers around it as hard as I could and made my wish.

The gas started cascading down from the old pipes, swirling around us, and the children began coughing and falling. The buttons rolled from their upturned palms onto the green floor—flowers in a meadow. Kiki stopped breathing. I began to lose the feeling in my body as I sensed my spirit drifting up and away, into the mist. I didn't resist it, because in the distance I could see my parents walking hand-in-hand, and a grinning apple-cheeked Milla Mouse on Mom's hip. The black emptiness in my stomach disappeared, and I felt light. One part of me hit the floor, and I saw the button rolling away from me, as if in slow motion. It wheeled towards the wizard, who had also fallen. While one part of me hit the hard floor, the other part slowly lifted and walked towards my family on the BrightSide, walked so lightly that I became one with the whirling white gas.

2

COLD BREATH

I knew why I deserved to be haunted by them, but I didn't understand why they, in particular, had chosen me.

I began noticing subtle signs of them, not knowing what their presence meant or where they came from. On my way to work one evening, I unlocked the front door and found a pair of little girl's shoes on the front step. Small, silver, scuffed on the sides and heels, with grey bows on the front. I didn't recognise them. They looked too small to be Kristina's, who was fast approaching nine years old. Eleanor, my wife, would get frustrated with me for not paying enough attention to Kristina. I should have known what time she finished school. I should have known what day she had soccer practice. She was a troubled girl, and I needed to pay more attention. I should have known if the shoes belonged to our daughter, but I did not.

The sudden presence of the shoes puzzled me, set out so neatly on the stone step. Kristina was already fed, bathed, and in bed, so I knew she had not put them there. After inspecting them, I put them back and drove to the hospital's ambulance bay, ready for my shift. When I returned home twelve hours later, the shoes were gone.

There was also a smell. A scent so subdued that in the beginning, I was sure I imagined it. It wasn't always the same, so it added to my uncertainty. Perhaps my sense of smell was just changing with age. When I asked Eleanor if she could smell it, she'd sniff the air dramatically and say *no*.

"What kind of smell?" she'd ask, genuinely interested.

I didn't know how to describe it. It was sweet and repulsive at the same time, and it kept changing. Dried flowers, chlorine, fresh bread. It got stronger over time, but Eleanor's answer was always no. After a while, I stopped asking.

The scuffed shoes. The odd smells. Then the nightmares started. Being a paramedic, my brain had no shortage of gory material to taunt me with while I slept. I'd always had bad dreams in one way or another—always had demons, even before I started the job—but the visceral nature of emergency medical care ramped up the intensity of the details, and the fright attached to experiencing them. It was very hard on me when I lost a patient; I'd think about them for days, obsessing about what I should've done differently, what I could have done faster. Losing patients made me feel worthless and out of control. I'd feel like nothing. Less than nothing; a cold breath. You'd think you'd get used to the trauma you see, but you don't. The nightmares became so realistic that I'd wake up in a cold sweat, my swollen heart skipping. I think when your job is to save lives, it becomes such a big part of who you are that the anxiety stays with you always, even in your dreams. You're always racing to save John Doe's life. Even in your sleep you're stripping the paper off syringes with your teeth, plunging needles, tying tourniquets. You're always trying to stop the bleeding, the relentless flow of blood.

The nightmares leaked into my days. I started seeing blood when I was awake, too. A smudge on the bathroom cabinet mirror; a fingerprint on the kitchen counter. When I saw the blood, my breath caught.

Did you cut yourself?" I asked Eleanor, and then Kristina. They both
shook their heads.

There's blood on this counter." But when I looked down again, it had
disappeared. I blinked hard, but it was gone. My wife and daughter
looked at me and then at each other, making wide-eyed faces.

He's finally lost it, I could imagine them thinking. *It was just a matter
of time.*

I made them scrambled eggs and toast. Eleanor liked her toast cold
and crunchy, so you had to wait for it to cool before buttering it. Kristi
would only eat toast if the butter had melted into it. I didn't mind. I
enjoyed their quirks, and it made me happy to see them enjoying the
food I had prepared. I loved seeing them sitting together, talking, legs
swinging under the table. They were close. We were a close family,
despite our troubles. I cleaned up the kitchen, polished the counter,
but the fingerprint stayed in my head all day.

Later that week I was leaning against the kitchen island scrolling my
newsfeed when I sensed a presence in the adjacent room. Eleanor was
at work, Kris at school. I looked up and got such a shock that I dropped
my phone, and it smashed on the tiles, splintering my screen. A small
girl was standing there, staring at me. She was drenched, as if she had
just come in from a storm, or was pushed into a swimming pool. Her
straight brown hair hung limply on either side of her pale face, dripping water on the floor along with her sopping green dress. I recognised the smell; it was one that I had come to know. She just stood
here, dripping, her eyes drilling into mine.

I blinked hard again, as I had done to the bloody fingerprint, hoping
she would disappear. She did, but the chlorine scent remained, and
the floor where she had been standing was wet. I picked up my shattered phone. I had wanted her to disappear, but now that she was gone

I wanted her to come back. I wanted to ask her who she was and why she had come. But did I really want to know? I couldn't help thinking she was there to punish me.

Deep down I knew I was sane, but I couldn't help questioning my state of mind. If I had imagined her, why had I done so? Maybe needed to cut down on my night shifts. Maybe I needed to cut down on my work in general. I needed a good night's sleep. I felt my anxiety swirling around the room like a grey tornado, ready to suck me into its violent vortex. I looked down at the tiles, and the puddle was still there.

A name popped into my head. Perhaps I just made it up, but it suddenly seemed clear to me. That was my first visit from Rosemary. She had looked around five years old, and she never seemed to age, she never changed her dress, and she never lost that intense look in her eyes.

Rosemary became a more frequent visitor. Sometimes it would just be the smell or an inexplicable splash of water. Some days there was sudden chill in the room, and the hair on the back of my neck would stand up. I'd close the bathroom cabinet and see her reflection there standing behind me, staring with those black lasers, and I'd jump foot in the air.

There was no opportunity to adjust to the situation because it quickly deteriorated. I signed up for fewer shifts at work but found myself not wanting to spend time at home, so I'd drive around the city, and there was just too much time to think. The tin top became claustrophobic. used to stop at the side of the road and climb out, just so that I could breathe. My insomnia took my sleep hostage. When I did manage to drift off, I had begun to talk—and sometimes walk—in my sleep. Eleanor had told me I was calling out other women's names. As you can imagine, that didn't go down well.

"Who the hell is Claire?" she asked one morning, slamming her toothbrush into the jar.

I just shrugged. What could I say? I could hardly tell her that Claire was a seven-year-old who had cracked glasses and a fatal head contusion.

We were short on money because I was working less, and for the first time in twenty years we missed a house repayment and got a call from our bank.

It was a tricky conversation. How do you tell the bank employee that a little drowned girl is haunting you, derailing your life? How do you tell him your wife has threatened to leave you and take your daughter with her if you didn't pull yourself together?

"It's not because I don't love you," Eleanor had said. "It's just that I think you need an ultimatum so that you can get your shit together."

After a long night of red wine and deep conversation, we agreed I needed help. We knew an excellent psychologist, Doctor Scott, who had helped Kristina a great deal with her emotional issues. Under Doctor Scott's care, she had stopped lashing out at us and stopped self-harming, although she still had breathing fits, and her imaginary friends.

"There's something she's not telling me," Scott had said. "Some trauma I can't access."

Eleanor and I agreed I'd see him as soon as I could. Eleanor even called the psychologist's office and set up the appointment for me, but I never went. How could I? I was afraid of what we might uncover. Eleanor set up another one, and I missed that one, too. Furious, she told me to pack a suitcase. When I did, feeling equally bereft and relieved, she cried and told me I was being stupid, and unpacked the bag.

"Dad," said Kristina, pulling on my sleeve. "Please. You need help."

Our eyes met. I couldn't bear the pain I saw there. It was like a vacuum, trying to swallow me.

I sat down and wept openly in front of them.

"I'm sorry," I sobbed. "I'm so sorry."

There were horrors deep inside me that were trying to claw their way out, and I was exhausted from keeping them inside. Kris looked at me then with something akin to hatred, and it seared my insides. My tears blurred my eyesight, and when I looked at Kristina again she was gone, and Rosemary sat in her place, leaking water into the couch. I wiped my eyes with the heels of my hands, and they had swapped again. I had my daughter back.

One by one, over the next few days, the other girls began appearing. Different girls, different ages, different clothes. In the end, there were seven of them. They all had their own particular smell and what I called a *wound*. Rosemary in the green dress was always wet; I guessed she had drowned. Susannah had a bullet wound in her chest, the blood of which stayed red and wet, so I wondered if the phantom fingerprints were hers. Coraline had blue lips and skin the colour of flour. She used to retch into her clammy, cupped hands, so I assumed she had ingested some kind of poison. It was too late to save their lives. I tried to talk to them, but they never answered my questions. I thought they needed my help.

"I can help you," I said to Susannah one day. "I can help all of you. If you tell me what you need. I can pass on your messages."

It soon became apparent that they were not there for my help, but they did have a message for me.

I was making a ham and cheese sandwich in the kitchen. It was part of a concerted effort to get some nutrients into my body; my appetite had disappeared, and I was losing weight at an alarming rate. I rinsed the bread knife and placed it on the drying rack. When I turned around, a bite had been taken out of my sandwich. Ice water trickled down my spine.

"Kris?" I called. "Eleanor?" but the kitchen was empty. I heard a scuttle at my feet and jumped. When I looked down, I saw blue-lipped Coraline there, squatting at my feet, holding a fork. As our eyes met, she gritted her teeth and jammed the fork into my thigh. The pain was immediate. I howled. It was a nasty, sharp, stinging sensation, but that's not why I cried out. I yelled in fear, because suddenly and with absolute clarity, I understood that the dead girls were there to harm me.

I removed the fork and cleaned the wound. I didn't even have to think about first aid anymore; my body just went into autopilot. The punctures were deep, but they soon stopped bleeding, so I applied an antibiotic ointment and a cartoon plaster. I couldn't bring myself to eat the sandwich, so I threw the tainted thing away. I acted calm, but my mind was rushing with panic. The dead girls weren't here for my help; they wanted me to suffer.

I sat down on the couch, my head in my hands, thinking hard. Where had they come from? It occurred to me that they may be former patients who I was unable to save, but I knew for sure that wasn't the case. I would have recognised them. I would have been haunted by them long before they had begun haunting me.

That night as I tossed and turned, I felt a cold breath, and then a hand on my shoulder. I turned toward it, thinking it was Kris, and held it tenderly in my hand. It was cool. Too cool. My eyes shot open and I saw Claire there, staring at me with giant pearls for eyes. I screamed and scrambled back, bumping into Eleanor who woke up with a fright and switched on the bedside lamp. As light flooded the room, Claire was gone. Of course she was. Static buzzed in my ears; my blood pressure made my temple throb. When Eleanor saw me, she screamed and fell out of bed, crabbing away from me. I looked at my hands. I was holding the bread knife. I dropped it as if it had burnt me.

"I don't know where it came from," I said.

Eleanor's mouth opened, but she couldn't talk.

"I don't remember getting it," I said. "I must have been having a nightmare. I must have sleep-walked."

She still couldn't say anything. She just held her hands up at me as if that could halt my spiral into insanity.

"I'm sorry," I said, but the words stuck in my throat because it was constricted with fear and my mouth was so dry. We stared at each other in horror.

Eleanor finally spoke. "This can't go on."

I nodded. She was right, of course she was.

"I think this house is haunted," I said.

"It's not the house that's haunted."

I looked away, my limbs trembling.

"You're seeing Doctor Scott tomorrow." Her face was as pale as linen, even in the warm artificial light of the lamp. "I'll make an emergency appointment for first thing in the morning."

"Thank you," I said.

"And let me be very clear about this." Her voice was shaky. "If you skip this appointment with Scott, I will have you committed."

"What?"

"I've been speaking to him since you missed your last meeting. He knows about what's been happening, how it's been escalating. He has a room for you at the psychiatric hospital in Killarney and an ambuance to take you there. I'm going to tell him about the knife, and if you miss this appointment they will come and collect you, and you will be committed. Do you understand?" Her lips were thin and dry, her eyes desperate.

blinked at her. "I'll see the doctor, first thing," I said. "I promise. I'll see im."

Eleanor grabbed the knife off the bed and took her pillow, then tomped out of the room. I guessed she would sleep in Kristina's bed.

The morning seemed aeons away. I lay awake, listening to my erratic heartbeat, waiting for the next dead girl to attack.

finally fell asleep when the sun began to rise. I felt safer, even though he dead girls didn't seem to care what time of day or night it was. When I woke up, I saw it was already close to midday, and a bolt of anxiety shot through me. I had missed my appointment with Doctor Scott. I leapt out of bed. I checked my phone, but it wouldn't switch on. I swore out loud and kicked the wall. Eleanor would have texted me the details of the appointment. I jammed the phone into the charger, but the screen didn't light up. I checked the port, the plug and the switch, but none of them seemed to be faulty. My shattered phone was the problem.

really was willing to see a therapist; it hadn't been an empty midnight promise. I needed to tell someone about the dead girls. I looked down at my legs and saw the bandaid there, and peeled it off. There were four neat puncture marks, well on their way to healing. The girls were real. The danger was real.

wanted to phone Eleanor, but we didn't have a landline telephone. All I had was my broken smartphone that refused to turn on. I could feel my sweat sticking my sleep shirt to my skin. I went into the bathroom to splash some cold water on my face, and it helped to clear my head. As I towelled off, I told myself that it was going to be okay. One way or another, I was going to get help, and we could go back to being a close family. But when I moved the towel away from my eyes and looked up, there were words written on the cabinet mirror. They hadn't been there before. Startled, I looked around the bathroom certain that one of the girls would be there yielding a razor or similar but there was no one there. I dragged my eyes back to the mirror to read the words written in blue marker.

LEAVE HER ALONE.

I may as well have been electrocuted at that moment, so deep and resonant was the bright shock that speared me right through my body. I fell to the white tiles below, hugging my knees to my chest like a frightened child.

No, I thought to myself. *No. They cannot know.*

When I had regained some strength, I stood up, but my legs were shaking. I felt weak and lightheaded. As if in a trance, I walked to Kristina's room. Her bed was neatly made, and there was a worn teddy bear on her pillow. I picked it up and put it to my nose, breathing in the scent I knew so well. I began to search her cupboards, and in the second last drawer of the ivory painted chest I found the blue marker. I blinked hard, but it did not disappear. I grabbed it and slid the bottom drawer open. Kris's personal five-year diary was there. Slowly, methodically, with trembling fingers, I untied the ribbon.

The pages smelled of the dead girls. Dried flowers. Chlorine. Gun powder. And there they were: seven names scribbled in blue marker on various dates.

Rosemary.

Susannah.

Coraline.

Kelly.

Abigail.

Fran.

Claire.

Only when I saw them written down like that did I put it together in my head. Eleanor always said I never paid enough attention to Kristina, but I recognised the names, then. I felt a presence in the room and a cold pocket of air. When I looked up from the diary, I expected to see one of the dead girls, but instead I saw Kristina. She had blue ink on her hands.

"Hello, Daddy," she said. She had that vacant expression she sometimes gets.

My body felt faint with rushing memories and thoughts and excess adrenaline. When I stood up, there were stars in my vision, half blinding me.

"Kristina," I said.

I heard the ambulance outside, and doors slamming. Heavy footsteps as the men entered the house, ready to subdue a man who had just lost everything.

I could hear them coming for me. I had been in an ambulance thousands of times, but never as the patient. Never as the person restrained on the stretcher.

"I don't understand," I said, but as the words left my mouth the realisation sunk in. Our matching memories hung in the air between us. The seven times I had suffocated her and brought her back to life. The swim in the sea, the pillow, the bath, the comforter. I thought she'd be too young to remember. I had made her heart stop and then I had restarted it. It made me feel powerful beyond measure. I wasn't a murderer, I told myself. My daughter is still alive. I couldn't save all my patients, but I could save her. Like the tide of the ocean, I passed her to the other side, and then I brought her back. Deep down I knew that one day it would go too far. The dead girls knew that, too.

The men in starched white uniforms burst in and overpowered me, hauling me away.

"Your imaginary friends," I said to Kris. "They came here to protect you."

It was too late for them, but it wasn't too late for Kristina.

"How?" I asked. "How did they get here?"

She stared as the men dragged me away.

"Every time you killed me," my daughter said, "I brought someone back."

~

3

THE CURSE OF STONE

Written by the (fictional) MillenniarellaBot AI after being fed classic fairytales and American stand-up comedy.

(Inspired by "The Christmas on Christmas" by Keaton Patti, who fed his bot thousands of Hallmark Christmas screenplays and then instructed him to write his own.)

∾

Once upon a time there lived a cold queen who was as beautiful as an Alaskan husky-hound and as cruel as minimum wage. She'd pay you in snow if it weren't illegal.

"I need a man," she said. "I need him to curse me."

Her bed was made of icicles, and her baby pouch was made of stone. It was like carrying around an iceberg in an apron made of skin.

The royal advisor was a crone, short and old as a tree trunk. You could count the centuries on her face.

"Come here," said the queen. "I want to count the centuries on your face."

"Stop your lip-noise," said the advisor. "You need a man to curse you."

"I have a plan," said the queen, and applied red mouth wax and tightened the laces of her breast-corset until she felt desirable.

"You don't know how to seduce the wolves," said the crone. "Your face is a bowl of sadness."

"I need to shape up for summer," said the queen, looking into her magic mirror which was not doing the right job. "I need to eat less and exercise more."

"Even the deadbeat ghetto birds think you are too cold," said the crone.

"I will eat them in a pie," said the queen. A lightning bolt smashed into the castle and zinged through the stone walls. Some of the turret guards outside were electrocuted by the sky-blast and tumbled into the moat below. The surviving guards pointed and laughed. The wrong-job mirror cracked in half ... he's in therapy now.

The queen smiled; she felt curse-worthy now. Her eyes were ice-cubes with lashes.

The old advisor was still breathing. She bent over into a question mark. "What is your plan?"

"I'll go to a restaurant that serves breakfast at any time and ask for Eggs Benedict during the Industrial Revolution."

"That sounds good," said the crone, picking her teeth with the sharpened edge of her magic wand. "That is a good plan."

The queen arrived at the deli and went straight to the sandwich counter. There was a man counting sandwiches.

I need a man to curse me."

The man looked confused but happy, like a hungry parking meter.

The queen put her frost-hands on the counter. "But first I need bacon."

You are my kind of queen," said the sandwich man.

The queen looked deep into the man's eyes. "It's easy to be confident when you have a full head of hair."

I like the way you wear your red mouth wax."

This plan is succeeding," said the queen. "I can feel it in my baby pouch."

Please be patient. I will get your bacon."

Don't forget the factory sauce," said the queen. "It must taste like smoke and ashes and small children stuck in chimneys."

The sandwich man brought the queen her Eggs Benedict, generously seasoned with sweatshop tears and sprinkled with soot.

The bacon is average," the queen said, wiping her mouth with her dreams.

The man was pleased; he recognised a compliment when he heard one.

Do you need marriage with your breakfast?" asked the sandwich man.

Will I need to pay double?"

He thought about it for a while and then nodded. They shook hands.

I believe in the idea of marriage," said the man. "I'll keep trying till I get it right."

"Look," she said, showing him the world inside her purse. "I have enough money to last us the rest of our lives."

"Yes," he agreed. "Unless you buy something."

A man of the cloth arrived with two suits.

"You should never trust a preacher with more than two suits," said the man.

"God is a squirrel," said the queen.

"God is not a squirrel," said the pastor. "He is just an underachiever."

"You are a precious frozen thing," said the sandwich man to the queen. "For this reason, I will not put you in my pocket."

The salad garnishes began to shiver and dance; the cherry tomatoes were pinballs.

"Let us begin the marriage," said the sandwich man. "This queen is cold and needs a man to curse her."

"Here," said the pastor. "Take these magic mushrooms."

"No thank you," said the queen. "I've already had bacon."

"Then drink this lemonade. It is LSD."

The old crone walked into the deli. "If you drink the open-mind juice you'll see that all matter is one."

"Yes," said the pastor, leaning on the counter and taking a bite out of crustless tuna mayonnaise sandwich. "Life is only a dream, and we are the imagination of ourselves."

"I can't drink the open-mind juice today," said the queen. "It will be bad for the curse."

"I like the centuries on your face," said the sandwich man to the crone.

"She is my greatest godmother," said the queen. "We couldn't decide if we should bury or cremate her, so we let her live."

"Death is not real," said the pastor. "She doesn't exist. Even if you wish she did."

"Has the marriage begun yet?" asked the sandwich man.

"It feels like it," said the queen. "Will you curse me now?"

"The sandwich man can't curse you," said the greatest crone. "You are a bag of cheap party ice, and your baby pouch is made of stone."

The queen began to cry. The tears hailed down her cheeks, shooting to the floor and rolling like ice marbles on the freshly swept linoleum. The man took her in his arms and kissed her, and the queen began to defrost. He yanked off his sandwich apron and cursed her three times.

The queen's baby pouch warmed and softened and turned into flesh, and in that flesh-balloon a baby began to grow like a magic bacon bean. The deadbeat birds arrived to sing. The pastor threw black pepper in the air, and they all sneezed. The greatest godmother danced to the ghetto birdsong, which was cheerful because they liked not being in a pie. The pastor swung the old crone around and kissed her skin-centuries.

For the first time in her life, the queen felt warm. Settling into the sandwich man's arms, she felt the curse swell inside her.

And they all lived happily ever after.

～

4

THE GREEN SILK SCARF

hanks for coming in," says Captain De Villiers, standing up and rubbing his stubble. He's looking rougher than usual, more unkempt. His face is as crumpled as his shirt. What he really means is: *Thank you for not making me come and get you from that damned sheep farm of yours, all the way in the* fokken *Free State.*

"You promised me we'd catch a wife-killer," Robin Susman says. "How could I resist?"

"Usually you're bloody good at resisting," says De Villiers. "You must be getting soft in your old age."

"Speak for yourself." Susman eyes the box of Calmettes on his desk. Since when did Devil need tranquillisers? De Villiers follows her gaze and scoops the pills off the table, dropping them in the open drawer below and slamming it shut.

"They're natural," he says, under his breath. Susman doesn't reply. She assumes the captain's wife has insisted on them. The Devil she knows is not one for herbal remedies.

"If the case is so open-and-shut, why do you need me?" Susman asks.

Khaya suddenly appears at the door. "You're back!" He grins at her but knows not to hug. Hugging comes with the risk of being stabbed by a ballpoint pen. Robin Susman has boundaries.

She nods. "Sergeant."

"I've just made the captain some coffee," Khaya says, passing it to Devil. "Would you like some?"

Susman laughs. "From this place? No. Thank you."

De Villers takes a sip and pulls a face. "Good call."

"You guys need to get with it," says Susman. "You need a decent coffee machine. I live on a farm in the middle of nowhere. I churn my own butter for God's sake ... and yet even *I* have a proper espresso maker."

"Certainly," says Devil, batting his short brown eyelashes and gesturing at the grubby surroundings. "Shall we order the gold-plated one, to match the rest of the office?"

Robin doesn't have to look around to capitulate. She knows by touch the thin walls, the cheap furniture, the broken ceiling fan that has been hanging skew for years. No matter how hot it becomes in the confined space, the officers know to never switch it on, or face the imminent threat of decapitation. Susman sighs. She knows there is no budget for anything; as it is, the police station is critically understaffed and has been for years.

But what do you do when a woman is missing? There's no time to complain about slow software or cracked windows. You just get on with the job. And in a city like Johannesburg, there is no shortage of missing persons cases.

Robin sits down, and Captain De Villiers passes her the file. MEGAN ELIZABETH SHAW.

Shaw disappeared two weeks ago. Both her husband and parents reported her missing when she didn't come home on the night of the 22nd of May. The husband—David—had seen her that morning and said she was her usual self. Nothing out of the ordinary.

Susman pages through the file, reading snippets as she listens to Devil's brief. There is a photo of Megan Shaw: brunette, average height, hazel-eyed and friendly-looking. She was wearing heavy makeup and a spotted silk scarf knotted at the neck.

"She looks like a film star from the 50s," says Susman, picturing those actresses who would don cat's-eye sunglasses and wrap their hair in a designer scarf before riding in an open-top sports car somewhere in California or St. Moritz.

"It's in her profile," says Khaya. "The scarves. Her friends say she had —and I quote—a 'scarf addiction'. Her mother said she'd never have left them behind. That's how she knows Shaw didn't leave on her own accord; when we checked her house, the scarves were all there."

"How would she know? That they were all there?"

"Marie Kondō," says the sergeant.

Susman frowns. "What now?"

"Ha," says De Villiers. "I had the same reaction. Shaw's mother said that the weekend before her daughter went missing, she had helped her sort her closets."

"Decluttering," says Khaya. "It's trending hard right now."

"They had given away all but her favourite scarves, and kept fifty."

"*Fifty*," said Khaya, giving her a pointed look, as if owning fifty scarves was scandalous. "And when we checked her place out, there were forty-nine. She was wearing her favourite one—green silk—the day she disappeared."

Susman began tapping the leg of the desk with her boot. "Remind me why this is significant?"

"Because she never packed a bag. Her toiletries are all still there. And she never packed any of her scarves."

"Sounds to me as if you guys are reaching."

Khaya stares at her. "So you think she *did* do a runner?"

"I don't think anything yet. All I'm saying is basing a case on a silly scarf seems sketchy at best."

"But you always say—"

"I know what I always say."

Susman always says *The Husband Did It*. Most of the time, she's right.

Blom sticks his head through the doorway, and his face lights up when he sees Robin.

"Susman!" he says. "Can I make you some coffee?"

"I'm getting the feeling you guys actually don't want me to stay."

Khaya laughs, showing off his perfect teeth.

"I have news," says the tall Dutch detective who they call *The Flying Dutchman.*

"Body?" asks De Villiers.

"*Negatief,*" says Blom. He's chewing gum, and Robin watches as his jaws work away at it. "I finally got through the red tape. They released her bank statements to us. Megan Shaw withdrew all her money the day before she disappeared."

Robin sits up a little straighter. "That's interesting."

"All her money?" Devil has a sip of his coffee and then has a regretful expression.

"Every cent. Savings, current, access bond, you name it. She maxed her cash withdrawal and sent the rest to PayDay. It's an international payment service based in the US. We can't access those records."

"Yet," says Devil. "Get on it."

"Yes, Captain." Blom retreats, giving Susman a wave. Khaya leaves, too.

"I don't understand why they're always so bloody happy to see you," moans De Villiers.

"Oh, please," says Susman. "They get to look at my face instead of yours for a few days. I'm surprised they're not throwing a party."

Devil purses his lips.

"Where is the husband?" asks Susman. "David Shaw. I'd like to speak to him."

When Robin Susman had been a detective in Devil's squad, she had cracked suspects in half with her interrogation technique.

It's not a technique, she used to say. *I just ask questions.*

That's what life's about, though, isn't it? Devil had said in one of his more reflective moments. *Asking the right questions.*

"I've tried already," he says. "Shaw doesn't answer a thing. Just says he's innocent and hides behind his attorney."

"Smart," says Robin.

"He was willing to do a lie-detector test."

Susman looks up at him.

"He passed. We're holding him, but don't have anything. Not really.

We're going to have to charge or release him in a few hours, and we're running out of time." He reaches for his jacket. "Want to go for a walk?"

They stride over the broken paving of the sidewalk, stepping over tree roots and potholes. Susman trips over the nub of a tree stump, and De Villiers catches her hand without thinking. She regains her balance and snatches it back.

"Sorry," he says. She thanks him in an annoyed way and plunges her hands back into her pockets and they keep walking.

Pigeons, pecking at the stale breadcrumbs near an overflowing rubbish bin, look up at them and scatter. Cars dodge and overtake, and aggressive drivers lean on their horns. Robin can taste the carbon monoxide in the air. Farm air is not without its stink, but she'd take compost and sheep dung over exhaust fumes any day.

"Nice to get some fresh air," jokes Devil.

Susman smiles at him, the sun's glare reflecting off the traffic and making her eyes water. "Tell me about the blood spatter."

"No blood spatter," says De Villiers.

They dodge weeds, rocks, and loose gravel. There is graffiti on the dirty brick walls, and an old empty chip packet glints as it's pushed along by the lazy breeze.

"I want a new forensic team checking her house."

"I can't authorise that. We don't have the budget." De Villiers runs his fingers through his hair. "Strictly speaking, we can't afford you on this case, either."

Susman stops walking to look him in the eye. "And yet, here I am."

The duo stand inside Megan and David Shaw's lounge. The captain's compromise was to get a junior forensic to comb the house again, and Susman could do her own search. After ninety minutes of careful inspection, they agree the lounge is clean. In Susman's mind, it's suspiciously clean. Susman snaps her latex gloves off to give her perspiring hands some air.

"Satisfied?" asks Devil.

"No."

Susman makes her way to the bedroom the couple shared and carefully looks through their things. She uses her borrowed UV light to check for blood residue, spraying Luminol as she slowly works through the room. The carpet smells of shampoo, the walls were recently scrubbed. Robin stops when she sees the scarf collection. Taking out her phone, she records a voice note saying how she thinks the room is too clean.

"Susman!" De Villiers calls. "We may have found something."

Susman turns to leave, but something is still bothering her. She spins around and looks again, her eyes scanning the room.

"Susman!" yells Devil.

Robin remembers the hairline crack in the clay stand of the bedside lamp. A sign of a struggle? She walks towards it, picks it up, and looks at the bottom. She doesn't need the Luminol to see the blood spatter. It's there: a fine spray of brown on the grey felt.

She wends her way back to the captain and the junior forensic.

"It might be nothing," says the intern, holding up a sealed evidence bag. It looks empty. "But we found what looks like female hair on the husband's outbound dry-cleaning. It was in the closet near the front door, ready to go."

"Long and blonde," adds Devil. "So, in other words, not his wife's."

"Good work, Junior," says Susman. "Now come upstairs, and bring your UV light."

They uncover three more patches of blood spatter: in the central light fitting, behind the wall-heater, and underneath the closet door.

"Someone cleaned this up really well," says the junior.

"Not well enough," says De Villiers, looking grumpy. Maybe he was disheartened that his original team had not found anything. Maybe he needs to be harder on them. Robin can tell he's been distracted lately.

While the forensic packs up the samples and the rest of his kit, Susman looks out of the window at the peaceful suburban scene outside. Indigenous trees, green lawns, kids riding bikes, and thinks what an illusion it all is.

"It's probably enough to charge him," says Devil. "But not to prosecute. No body, no motive, no weapon."

"An outsider wouldn't have gone to so much trouble to clean up."

De Villiers nods in agreement.

"The blonde hair could point to the motive," says Susman. "Let's find out who the owner is."

While the evidence is being processed in the lab, Blom arranges for David Shaw's car—a silver Audi—to be searched. The report comes back clean. Devil orders a second search. Again, the report is clean.

"Anything on the DNA of that hair yet?" De Villiers yells into his hone, then shakes his head. After he ends the call, he slams his phone n his desk. "Blood is hers," he shouts, and the office goes quiet; an nintended minute of silence for the victim. Robin doesn't feel the sual cold wash that accompanies these murder cases. Perhaps the ile of bodies has simply grown too high.

The mother just called," says Khaya. "The vic's mother. Said that Megan and David had an argument the night before she disappeared."

Blom chips in. "That's what the neighbour said, too. Said she heard hem shouting at each other. Said it happens often and they don't even all the cops anymore."

Had she ever laid any charges against him?" asks Robin. "Domestic iolence?"

No," says Khaya, "but the vic's mother said she'd often have bruises. Always had an excuse for them, though. Mother says that the vic's ather never approved of the marriage. So maybe she felt like she ouldn't tell them about the abuse."

But no evidence, right?" says De Villiers. "No broken bones or ospital records."

Right," said Khaya. "Just a mother's opinion."

We could put her and the neighbour on the stand," says Susman. But it's a bit patchy."

Is the blood spatter enough to charge him with?" asks Blom, glancing t his watch. "We've got an hour left before those clerks start packing p."

Oh," says Khaya, scratching his head with the back of a cheap yellow en. "She also said to check his *bakkie*. A Ford Ranger."

His *bakkie*?" asks Blom, unfamiliar with the South African slang.

His pickup truck," says Khaya.

"You should know that by now," says Devil. "You bloody Dutchman."

"Talk about the pot calling the kettle black," says Robin.

"Who are you calling black?" jokes Khaya.

They laugh, but not for long.

"Okay," De Villiers says. "Khaya's checking on the *bakkie*. Blom i
going to nag the lab." He drums his fingers on his desk so hard they a
stare at him. "Go on," he says to Khaya and Blom. "Get lost. I need t
think."

Once the officers leave, Robin gets a faraway look in her eyes. "I
would explain the heavy makeup. And the scarves."

Devil rubs his temples. "What?"

"You can hide bruises with scarves."

Devil watches as Robin's fingers unknowingly travel to her collarbon
They'd had to pin it back in place, if he remembers correctly, and i
hadn't been the only surgery she had required. He tries not to winc
His phone rings, making them both jump. He barks his name and the
listens intently as he scribbles notes on the back of a sheet. Robi
stands up and moves to look over his shoulder, trying to decipher hi
awful handwriting.

Cross, Hailey.

Nurse.

Knew vic.

Deal.

Immunity.

The last word was underlined, but Robin couldn't tell if it said *witne*
or *mistress*.

"Uh-huh," he says. "Uh-huh. Show her to the interview room. We'll be there in five minutes."

Hailey Cross is waiting in the grey room. She wipes her hands on her jeans before shaking Devil's hand. She's petite, moderately attractive, and has cascading blonde hair. She frequently swigs from a bottle of water she's brought along. Dry mouth, clammy hands. She's not even trying to hide the fact that she's as nervous as a cat in a cage. Her attorney sits, stone-faced and silent, beside her.

"Thank you for coming in to talk to us," says De Villiers. "I realise you don't get much time off—as a nurse—so we really do appreciate it."

Robin stares at him. She's never heard him be so polite in his life. Maybe the tranquillisers are working. Or maybe he was working on his manipulation technique.

"I heard that David's getting out this afternoon." Hailey's eyes dart nervously between them.

"Yes," says Susman.

She chews on her lower lip; her eyes have dark crescents beneath them. She hasn't been sleeping. "You can't let him go."

"We don't have enough evidence to charge him," says Devil.

"He did it," she says. "He murdered Megan. In their bedroom. He wrapped a jersey around her head and then smashed it with a baseball bat."

Robin shuddered. She gripped her knees in an attempt to silence her body's reaction to such brutality. Devil took the pen out of his mouth and blinked at the nurse. "How do you know this?"

Hailey Cross blew her fringe out of her eyes. "Because I was there."

. . .

"Why did you wait so long to come in?"

"I didn't want to be implicated," she says, looking at her attorney. "Accessory to murder? Obstruction of justice? But then I heard he was getting out—"

"—and you knew he'd come for you, next," says Susman.

"Yes." Hailey lifts a hand to her eyes and begins to cry. "I can't get it out of my head," she says, rubbing her forehead. "I just keep seeing it happen over and over again. And I know he'll do the same thing to me." She begins to unbutton her blouse, and the captain instinctively looks away. When his gaze returns to Cross, he sees a large bruise across her chest. She also shows them what looks like a cigarette burn on the inside of her forearm. "He is a vicious man."

By the time she has buttoned up, she has stopped crying.

"You were having an affair?" asks Robin, thinking of the long blonde hair they had found at the house.

Cross nodded. "We met a year ago. He wasn't wearing his wedding ring. When I found out about his wife, I tried to end the relationship. That's when he started beating me. I tried to leave, but he'd always find me. He enjoyed it." Her lips pulled to the side with emotion. "He enjoyed hurting me. Said if I ever went to the police, he'd kill Peggy, and I knew it was true."

"Peggy?"

"My Jack Russell. She's missing a leg," the nurse says, as a way of explanation. Devil looked confused, but Susman knew the common nickname for pets missing a leg. Peg-leg. *Three-leggy Peggy*.

"I knew he would do it," Hailey says.

"You were trapped," says Susman.

"I knew he would do it," she says again. "He's done it before."

"Killed an animal?"

"At the cabin," she says. "We'd go there, in the beginning, so that his wife wouldn't find out about us. It used to be romantic, but then it got scary. He knew he could do whatever he wanted to me in that cabin, because it's in the middle of nowhere, so—"

She doesn't have to say the rest. *So that no one could hear her scream.*

"God." Susman didn't mean to say it out loud. Her skin turns to braille.

"Why didn't we know he had a cabin?" asks Devil. "It would have been the first place we searched."

"It doesn't technically belong to him," said Cross. "I don't know the details—he was evasive—but as far as I know, it belongs to a friend of his. There'd be no paper trail."

"Tell us about Megan Shaw," Devil says. Susman looks at the clock on the wall. They have twenty minutes left to submit the charge sheet, and that's if the clerks don't take off early.

Hailey Cross takes a sip of water. "David wanted me to kill her."

There is silence in the grim, grey room as they process the information.

Devil frowns at her. "Why?"

"He said she was getting suspicious of us. He found out she was preparing to file a restraining order before starting divorce proceedings. David was furious that she was doing this behind his back, said she had betrayed him. He said she was going to take all their money and disappear. But if we killed her, we'd get all the money. And we could move somewhere and start again, and be happy."

"He wanted *you* to kill her?" Devil says.

"The neighbours knew they had a rocky relationship," she says. "If his

wife was going to disappear, he needed an alibi. He said that they—
that you, the cops I mean—always suspect the husband. And he
wanted me to prove myself to him. Prove my loyalty."

"What my client is failing to mention," says the attorney, finally
breaking his silence, "is that she was under severe emotional strain and
manipulation by a cunning and violent man. He told her he'd kill her
dog if she stepped out of line."

"We understand that," says Devil.

"So before we continue, I'd like to make a deal for her immunity from
prosecution in this case."

De Villiers rubs his stubble. "We're not charging her."

"Yet," says the attorney, not breaking eye contact. "But if you find her
DNA in the Shaw house—"

"Whether or not we charge her will depend on her culpability," says
Devil.

"Screw culpability," the attorney says. "She practically had a gun to
her head."

Devil grinds his teeth and looks at the clock, then transfers his gaze to
Hailey. "He'll be released today unless you start talking." Susman
doesn't know why he's playing hardball. Maybe it's because he doesn't
trust her. She'd witnessed a brutal murder, and it had taken her two
weeks to come in. Susman, on the other hand, could see the despera-
tion in the woman's eyes. Cross wasn't lying about the abuse, and that
was enough for her.

"Make the deal," Susman says. She thinks Devil will glare at her for
overstepping the mark, but he doesn't. Without hesitating, he affirms
the deal with Cross's attorney. He phones it in, as well as a call to
Khaya to file the charges against David Shaw. "Eye-witness account,"
murmurs Devil into his phone. Soon a flurry of papers arrive. He and

he nurse hurriedly sign them. They get submitted just in time to keep
haw behind bars, and Hailey Cross crumples in relief.

he sun sinks, and boxes of cold takeaway pizza lie in the middle of
he table. De Villiers had ordered dinner for them at his own expense,
ut no one is hungry.

I was supposed to spike her coffee," Hailey says. "Make it look like
he took an overdose. Then tape a plastic bag around her head in case
he woke up. I got the pills from the pain clinic where I work."

)e Villiers scrawls in his scuffed notebook.

David said I should buy her a takeaway coffee and stop by, to intro-
uce myself as a new neighbour."

Did you do that?" asks Susman.

I took her the coffee. We spoke. But I didn't put the sedative in it."

Why not?"

I'm not like that." Cross clasps her hands together. "I like to help
eople, not hurt them."

That bruise on your chest," says Susman. "That was because you
idn't kill her that day?"

David said I was disloyal. That he couldn't trust me anymore. He hit
ne with the baseball bat and then gave it to me, said now I'd have to
o it the hard way, or he'd kill Peggy, and then he'd kill me."

What did you do?" asks Robin.

heir eyes meet, and time seems to stutter between them. Then
Iailey blinks, breaking the tension. "I took the baseball bat."

. . .

"I went to her house on the 22nd of May," says Hailey. "I was scared of David, and I wanted his approval, but I just couldn't go through with it. I left the bat there, at the front door."

Robin can't put her finger on it, but it seems to her that something changes in the way Hailey is talking. Perhaps being a victim of abuse had caused her to disassociate to a certain degree on the day of the murder. Either that, or she was lying.

"I gave Peggy to someone I trusted and then called David to tell him it was over. He went ballistic. A few hours later he told me to meet him at his house."

"Why?" asked Susman.

"He said because I hadn't done my job, he'd had to do it. And the least I could do was clean up the mess."

That's why the room was so clean, thought Robin. *A nurse would know how to clean up blood.*

"It was horrific. It took hours," said Hailey. "It was everywhere. He asked me ... to find a tooth."

"What?" Susman clutched her knees again to stop from shuddering.

"Her tooth. He had knocked out one of her teeth but couldn't find it."

"And did you?" asks Susman. "Find the tooth?"

"Yes," says Cross, swallowing hard. "An incisor, with roots."

Silence again, as they process the grisly detail.

Devil clears his throat. "So you cleaned up the evidence. Where was David?"

"He took the body. Wrapped it up in the bloody bed sheet and got rid of it."

"How?"

"I haven't spoken to him since then," says Hailey. "But I can tell you the original plan—with the drugged coffee—was to take the body out to the cabin. I'll give you the address. He planned to burn it there and dump the ashes in the river. I don't know if he did that, but I'm guessing he would have. Not that there'll be any evidence."

"There's always evidence," says Devil.

The recently admonished forensic team arrives at the cabin before dawn and knuckles down, searching every square inch of the cabin and its surrounds. The autumn air is cold and makes their breath look like cigarette smoke. The backdrop is tall, black-barked trees and yellow leaves, and the ground is soft. The cabin has been searched twice already and found to be clean.

"If you don't find anything," the Devil yells. "You're all *fokken* fired!"

Susman laughs into her polystyrene cup, forcing a cloud of steam into the air.

Devil's phone rings. The Caller ID says *Sgt Sithole*.

"You're on speakerphone," says Devil.

"Hiya, Boss," says Khaya. The man was always in a good mood. Susman doesn't know how he does it. "We found the *bakkie*."

"And?"

"Do you want the good news or the bad news?"

Robin feels the wash of water inside her then, but not the cold flush that usually means the missing woman is dead. It's more like a slow dripping. Tap, tap, tap.

De Villiers rolls his eyes. Silhouettes of birds dart across the dawn sky. "Jesus, Sithole, just get on with it."

"I was only kidding," he says. "There's no bad news. We found something."

"We're listening," says Robin.

"A tooth. An incisor, with the root and everything, like you said. It was wedged in the crevice of the seat."

"Good," says Devil. "Good. Very good."

Just in case one "good" is not enough, thinks Robin. She pictures the crevices of couches and sofas and car seats the world over and wonders what treasures lie buried therein. Coins and toys and murdered women's teeth. Tickets to convict killers.

Devil ends the call. "So Hailey Cross is telling the truth."

"It looks like it," says Susman. She drains her cup and throws it in the nearby black plastic bag, a makeshift bin. His walkie talkie, which has been whispering to him all morning in static and garbled comments, blinks green.

"Captain," says the man on the other side of the two-way radio. "Captain. Come in. Over."

De Villiers snatches the radio from his belt. "I'm here."

"We're around five or six hundred metres down the river. The vegetation is quite thick. Difficult to navigate. But there's a metal trough here. Burnt. The river has done a good job of rinsing it out—it's been two weeks—but it might be something. We'll bring it up. Any sign of ash is long gone. Over."

"All right," says Devil. "But keep looking. All we need is one bone fragment."

How dreadful, thinks Susman. To be reduced to a single sought-after bone fragment in a rushing river. How sickening. She feels her heavy cloak pull down at her shoulders, but before Robin can give in to her despair, she spots the junior forensic striding towards them. When their eyes meet, he waves at her, a small evidence bag in his hand.

"Hey!" she says, happy to see him. If she were still on the force she would have snatched him up as part of her A team. She knows talent when she sees it.

He's out of breath, and there is perspiration on his forehead despite the cool air around them.

"The scarf Shaw was wearing that day," he says. "The day she went missing. It was green, right?"

Susman nods. He passes the sealed bag to her. Inside is a small swatch of fabric, green, silk, and burnt at the edges.

∼

THREE MONTHS LATER

Devil offers to pick Susman up from the airport, but she decides to drive up from the farm instead. It was only for one day, to watch the court proceedings of the state versus David Shaw for premeditated murder and obstruction of justice. De Villiers had kept her up-to-date via WhatsApp throughout the trial, and he was confident that Shaw would be convicted. Hailey Cross had held up her side of the deal and had been a star witness, remembering small details and never straying from her original gruesome testimony.

Relatives, officers and journalists filed in and a buzz of anticipation crowded the courtroom. Susman and De Villiers sat down on the wooden bench together, just behind the prosecutor. Susman notices Hailey Cross standing right at the back of the room, as if still afraid of David and ready to flee. When they lead the accused in, he looks like a broken man, and Susman doesn't feel an ounce of empathy for him.

For the last three months she had been haunted by the *CRACK!* of a baseball bat connecting with a feminine skull. Hitting it so hard that a whole tooth fell out. That, and the imagined smell of the fire in the blackened trough. How very coldblooded you have to be to burn your own wife's body in a sawn-off steel barrel.

Susman didn't have to be here. De Villiers would have let her know the verdict—he may have even splashed out and used a happy emoji in the message—*Looks like we caught our wife-killer* (: —but something had told Susman she should come through, and so here she sits, looking around at the eager faces around her.

The judge marches in and sits down with little fanfare. She doesn't need to ask the crowd for quiet; they all hang on her every word. She gives a short speech about how there's no doubt in her mind that the verdict they have reached is correct, and then, with a firm grasp of the paper in her hand, she reads the verdict. In the end there had been six charges, including premeditated murder, and she announces that the court had found David Shaw guilty of every one. When Robin turns to look at Hailey, she's gone. Susman stands up, and Devil follows. He's right behind her as they exit the courtroom buildings. They follow Cross, who is striding, and quickly jump behind an electricity box when she looks over her shoulder. Maybe she feels their eyes on her back.

They follow her three blocks north, where there is a large, run-down park. The low gum-pole fence is falling over, the grass needs mowing. People mill around. There are some dogs on leashes, and winos and beggars sleep in the shade. There is a public toilet with a skew door which Devil and Susman hide behind. They watch Hailey Cross meet a woman sitting on a bench in the dense shade of a huge mulberry tree. The woman stands and hugs Cross, passing her the red leash of a three-legged Jack Russell who is jumping and barking in excitement.

The woman is not wearing a scarf, but when she smiles widely at Cross, she reveals a missing tooth.

. . .

The truth rushes at Robin. The scenes play out in her head as if she's watching a jump-cut film. She may not have all the details right but she can imagine the story played out something like this: Under David Shaw's direction, his mistress, Hailey Cross, takes his wife coffee that day. She fails to use the sedatives in her handbag. The nurse sees that David's wife has bruises just like hers, and she confesses the affair. They bond over their shared trauma. They have to stop David Shaw before he kills one or both of them; they both know it's just a matter of time. Together, they hatch a plan. Megan will withdraw all her money and then precipitate one last row with David—accusing him of cheating—loudly enough for the neighbours to hear, thereby establishing a motive. Megan will raid her workplace —the clinic—for the things she'll need: hairnets, booties, local anaesthetic, syringes, needles. A bag and IV line to collect Megan's blood. Perhaps she stops at a hardware store to buy a plastic spray bottle and a pair of pliers, or maybe she gets them from her own garage. On the night of the 21st of May, Megan uses Hailey's stolen sedatives to drug David. While he's unconscious, she lets Hailey into the house, and they kit up and get to work, spraying the bedroom with the blood they had drained from Megan's arm, and then scrubbing around the evidence, being careful to leave just the right amount of blood. Hailey would have numbed Megan's gums with the anaesthetic and then pulled out the incisor, tucking it into David's car seat. Hailey would have given Megan the Jack Russell to look after. Megan would have disappeared, but not before going up to the cabin and burning her green silk scarf in the trough, making sure the wind blew some of the fragments into the surrounding trees. David would wake up with a headache, search for his wife, and then report her missing.

"*My fok,*" says Devil, rubbing his upper lip and then reaching for his handcuffs. "We need to take them in."

Susman can't tear her eyes away from the women under the Mulberr
tree, who are now parting ways. "Do we?"

Devil's hand freezes on the cuffs that are clipped to his belt. "O
course we do. David Shaw is innocent."

"No," Susman shakes her head as she watches the women hurriedl
leave the park. "He's not."

5

NOT WAVING

I *'m fine,* the woman told them.

I'm fine, the woman told herself.

As long as I keep treading water, I'll be fine.

Just keep treading. Just keep kicking. Keep your head above the water, and you'll be okay. But the water was getting colder, and darker. The waves were getting bigger. Fatigue slowed her muscles and exhaustion threatened to pull her under.

I'm fine, the woman told herself.

I still smile. Life is good. Life has never been better. I still joke. There's a lot to laugh about.

The children were smart and independent and loving. They were the best thing that ever happened to her. The six-year-old was quirky and wise beyond his years, the four-year-old had a huge heart and made up nonsensical knock-knock jokes, and the two-year-old was fierce and funny and full of love. There was a lot to laugh about, but the woman found herself laughing less and less.

Maybe it was her bank balance that was weighing on her. That wasn't so funny. Every time she saw a glimmer of hope that her books were selling, her life was working ... when she glimpsed her inevitable success she thought: *I was right, it's going to be okay. I always knew it was going to be okay.* Then she'd look at her hungry credit card and feel the shame flame her cheeks. No matter how hard she kicked, she was still going under.

It wasn't just the notes and coins and the numbers on the screen. Money was her security blanket. On good days it warmed her shoulders, on bad days she couldn't find it anywhere and felt bereft. Every time she built up a cushion of hope and finally rested on it, it got pulled from underneath her. Unexpected bills choked her. The money flowing away felt like fingers around her neck, slowly squeezing. Feelings of failure strangled her.

The scrutiny of strangers was nothing new. She'd always hated attention; would rather have spiders crawl over her body than speak in public. The spotlight made her sweat. As a pre-schooler, she chose to be spanked rather than participate in *Show & Tell.* They forced her to talk, forced her to eat, even when she retched.

Spanking and strawberry jam sandwiches. She still can't eat strawberry jam.

As a toddler she locked her mother out of the car before school, made her promise she'd never have to go back to the place that made her retch. The mother hid her under her desk at work until she found a better crèche.

The old jam-scented memories surfaced when the woman attended a meeting with her two-year-old's preschool teacher.

She won't speak to the class, the teacher said. *She doesn't like to be the centre of attention.*

The woman's stomach contracted. *Nor do I,* she replied. *Nor does my mother.* A genetic curse. Sometimes fear travels like disease through generations.

She'll come out of her shell, the teacher said. *She's only two.*

But the woman knew better.

The woman kept kicking, but she was getting tired. She realised she'd been exhausted for years. When she was pregnant with her third child, the obstetrician asked her how she was feeling.

Exhausted, she had replied.

He laughed. He had three kids of his own. He woke up at 3 am every weekday to prepare for surgeries and was on call 24/7.

You're not going to get any less exhausted, he said.

After seven years of cycling through infertility, pregnancy, breast-feeding and sleep deprivation, the woman sometimes felt that her body was nothing less than a miracle. In bleaker times she felt that it had been leached all the way down to the marrow; if you cut open her bones you'd find nothing but white sand.

The water was getting darker still. The woman would cope; she had always coped. She was naturally optimistic, persistent, resilient. She knew how to push herself; she knew how to achieve goals. She kept kicking. She thought she was fine, but then she realised her babies were in the water with her. Her sons could swim, but her daughter couldn't. The woman knew that you couldn't hold a baby and keep yourself afloat at the same time. Her sons were scared, hanging on to her and yelling. She couldn't hear what they were saying past the roar of panic in her head. They didn't mean to, but they were pulling her down. The two-year-old, terrified, began to scream.

. . .

The woman used to think the world was a safe place. (It's not.)

Danger is a swift enemy. You think you'll have time to react, to fend off the peril, but bad things happen quickly.

The woman's baby almost died.

The night before, the baby was running around with her brothers and eating pizza for dinner. The next morning her breathing was coming in short puffs. At the ER, the woman and the doctor fought with the baby, holding down her thrashing arms to insert the IV into her tiny vein. They plunged a needle into her thigh, pumping her body full of adrenaline. The paramedics were kind.

"Don't panic," they told the woman, setting out their intubation equipment in the ambulance. "We probably won't need this. But kids are unpredictable."

The woman stayed at her baby's side, holding her hand, stroking her head. Seven days and seven nights. She slept on a stretcher and showered in the middle of the night to make sure her daughter wouldn't wake up alone in the strange room. She nebulised the baby every six hours and called the nurses every time the child's breathing became laboured. They began to roll their eyes, but she didn't care.

There was some sad news. Their beautiful cat, a loyal friend of ten years, had died while the woman and child were being held hostage at the hospital. The woman paced the room, crying, feeling like she was going mad. Just a week before, life had been happy and full of hope. They'd just bought a bigger house. Book sales were climbing; the children were thriving. The woman felt too lucky. She had been right.

The woman cried when her baby got better, and she cried when her aby got worse. The tide rose and fell, rose and fell. She was a piece of roken driftwood being dashed against the rocks.

he baby railed against the perpetual IV line, the oxygen tubes plas-red to her nose. She wanted to leave the room, but she was a prisoner a her metal crib. Desperate, the screaming infant did everything she ould to escape. The woman pretended to be strong while her aughter was awake and wept into her soft muslin sheet while she ept.

was a long and slow process, but the baby recovered. Finally out of ne hospital, they spent hours together on the armchair while the oman held the nebuliser against her baby's nose and mouth. Trauma-sed, the child fought the medicine, as she had in the hospital. *It was uddle time,* the woman would say. *Storytime.* They both got used to . They had survived.

hey were still alive, but the woman felt as if she had been struck by ghtning. She had a constant echo in her head. It was wordless, but it lways held the same message.

he world is not a safe place.

he world is not a safe place.

he world is not a safe place.

he woman began seeing danger everywhere. She was living in a new eality where her brain was filled with the television screen static of nxiety. Headlines assaulted her. Polar bears starved to death. Nations lected predators to presidents and rape was a national sport. Men lot their fiancées in the face. The woman began to read less news, to rotect her state of mind, but it didn't stop the long-abused planet

being ravaged by flooding and fire. The stories and the bodies piled u
and she felt the weight of them on her shoulders and in her stomach.

She went to bed overwhelmed and woke up exhausted. Noises sta
tled her. The clang of a teaspoon dropping on the floor spiked he
adrenaline so hard she felt like running. Irritable and on edge, th
voices of her own children grated her. Being gradually eroded, sh
stopped dancing in the kitchen, stopped trying to make her kids laugl
She didn't answer the phone. Friends and family chatted and laughed
The woman laughed along, but deep down her mind was saying *Don*
you know my baby almost died?

I would have died, too.

But you don't say that in polite conversation. You don't say that whil
everyone's talking about power cuts and drought and travelling t
Panama and craft gin. While the woman's mind wandered to th
ambulance ride, the needles, the blood on her baby's pacifier.

On dark nights the woman sticks a needle into her own heart: *Yo*
should have taken her to the doctor sooner. You should have taken
stand with the nurses. You should have done more. If she had stoppe
breathing it would have been your fault. You are her mother.

The world is not a safe place.

My baby almost died.

I would have died, too.

The woman and her family survived.

They began to settle into their new house. The remaining ca
mourned her life-long friend for months. The woman sometimes felt
ghost feline wrap his tail around her legs, only to look down and se
nothing; just the shadows that had crept in, reminding her of her nev
dangerous world and the dark water.

The bigger house was wonderful and cursed at the same time. The pool was a warm oasis that would keep the children occupied for hours, and at the same time it was a cold black abyss that would haunt the woman's dreams; her baby drowning in it, over and over. The big, beautiful tree in the front garden she had fallen in love with while house hunting turned out to be infested with tiny moth-like insects that drifted down like snow in summer. The tree sprayed black all over the cheerful walkway, all over the white walls. During water restrictions, there was a leak beneath the house that cost thousands and thousands in lost water alone. In Cape Town, the drought was so dire that people were queuing for water. The knowledge twisted inside her. She couldn't look at the invoice; she was still hurting from the hospital bill. Because of the massive leak, the beautiful parquet flooring began to lift, the wooden tiles damaged beyond repair. The woman didn't want to guess what other devastation the water had wrought below the ground; she imagined that soon the whole house would collapse into a hole.

When it rained, the house was a sieve. The children would tear around, hunting for leaks. They would put down buckets, bowls, towels, bathmats. More timber tiles lifted. The grass died. The courtyard lemon tree was attacked by mould. The pool turned green.

Once, while the woman was working, there was a small movement in her peripheral vision. She looked across and saw a mouse scampering down the bannister. She had a sudden and irrational urge to burn the house to the ground.

We're just getting used to it, they told themselves and each other. *We'll be able to keep up with the maintenance soon.*

But the working hours were relentless and the children more so. The electric gate stopped working. Load shedding meant they'd go without electricity for hours every day. Sometimes, the water was cut off, too. Another burst pipe, this time under their driveway, which refused to be fixed. The woman fought the feelings of despair, but they fought back.

The children loved their new schools and grew like weeds. They always demanded more than the woman could give them. She loved them fiercely and without restraint. Her eyes pricked with tears when she hugged them goodnight and smelled their warm, sweet skin. They were everything, but they also took everything. *Stop growing,* she used to tell them.

I want you to stay small forever.

I want you to be mine forever.

I love you too much.

The days were long.

The woman and the man were in survival mode. Some days were easier than others. They would look at each other over their mugs of tea at night, relishing the silence of slumbering children, and say *It's getting easier, isn't it? They're such great kids. They're doing so well.*

Some days getting the children to school seemed impossible. Three mouths to feed, three bodies to wrangle, three sets of teeth to brush. Don't forget the sunscreen or the hats or the snacks or the library bag or *Show & Tell.* Don't forget to enjoy every moment because they're only small once. Late for school and rushing, the four-year-old threw a tantrum and refused to walk. The woman ground her teeth and forcefully strapped him into the pram and put the two-year-old on the wheelie board behind. The toddler didn't want to be there and kept hopping off until the woman forced her back on and scolded her with a violent whisper. They both began to howl. The six-year-old was upset; he was late for school. He was worried he'd get a black mark. Cars sped past them. It began to rain, and in her rush to leave the house, she had forgotten her umbrella. The woman's anxiety ramped

up to a new, all-time high. A stone burned in her throat. Don't forget
to enjoy every moment.

The woman focused on the good times. She reminded herself to
breathe, to spend time in nature. She led a privileged life and had little
reason to complain. She kept treading the water. Things were going to
get better.

The man complained of chest pain. The woman made him take an
aspirin. A year before, she wouldn't have worried—he was healthy and
in great shape—but the lightning bolt had taught her to fear. It's not
just children who are unpredictable. The pain went away for a week,
then came back late one night. They packed a hospital bag and called
an Uber. The woman wanted to go with her husband to the ER but
had to stay at home with the children, who were fast asleep in bed.
She paced the room, the office, the kitchen, waiting for his messages.
When she got tired of pacing, she sat and forced her adrenaline into
her work. She couldn't think straight. Finally, the text arrived. The
man was okay; his heart was fine. ECGs don't lie.

Stress? They wondered. *Panic attack? Acid reflux?* The man has
always been a Stressed Eric. He had a short emotional fuse and his
first ulcer when he was twelve.

The next time he had chest pain, they ignored it. It went away. When
it came back, it was more intense. He made an appointment with a
well-respected cardiologist, just for peace of mind. The consultation
was weeks away. They continued in survival mode. Had they ever not
been in survival mode? Wasn't that what life was, for most people,
anyway?

The pain didn't go away. On a bicycle ride in the middle of nowhere,
the man felt off-colour. The woman was worried but reminded herself

of the ECG. His heart was fine. The woman had three children pulling and hanging on her like nagging vervet monkeys. They were hungry, they were fighting, they needed a bath, they needed their mom. The woman didn't have time to worry about a healthy heart, so she pushed it down, pushed it down into the black water she was treading. In a parallel world, her husband was swimming at the gym in a pool so clear it looked like glass. When he pushed off under the water, he felt his heart squeeze.

The man remembered the story of an acquaintance who had died in a pool and then was slowly brought back to life. The man got out of the water.

The cardiologist consultation went well. The doctor was about to sign the clean bill of health when it came to the end of the stress test, where the man had to run on a treadmill, his strong-looking heart hooked up to the monitor.

"I didn't like what I saw at the end of the stress test," the doctor said on the phone to the woman.

What did he see?

"I just didn't like the way he looked. I want him to come in for an angiogram."

What could the woman say? She wasn't going to argue with one of the best cardiologists in the country. The doctor recommended doing it on that Friday. He had an anaesthetist ready to help, should he go ahead and book the procedure?

The man said no, he felt fine, after all, and he had an important meeting on Friday. The doctor pushed again for Friday, but the man booked it three days later, on the Monday morning.

· · ·

riday arrived, and it was time for the man to leave for the important
meeting. He put his helmet on, then took it off and sat on the couch,
rubbing his chest as had become his habit. He sprayed his new
medication under his tongue.

The cardiologist had said if he felt any heart pain, he was to use the
spray. If he needed to use it a second time, he must go straight to
the ER.

Don't wait to phone me," he had said. "Just get straight to the hospital
and call me on the way."

After the first spray, his chest pains were not abating. He sprayed
again. He felt better, and he put his helmet back on. The woman's
nerves were so shot she felt like her hair was on fire. She insisted her
husband listened to the cardiologist's advice. The man tried to call the
doctor but the line was busy.

I'll call him on the way," he said. He meant to the meeting, not
the ER.

At that moment, if there existed an insta-divorce app, the woman
would have used it.

He rode halfway down the block when his doctor called him back and
told him to meet him in surgery immediately.

The cardiologist called the woman a few hours later. "It's called a
Widow Maker," he said. "The most fatal heart attack you get."

The world is not a safe place.

During the angiogram, they discovered the man had a critical
narrowing of his left anterior artery, the most crucial pipeline of the
heart. If that gets blocked, your whole heart collapses.

"It wasn't a matter of IF he would have died," said the surgeon. "It WHEN he would have died."

Which, the woman thought, you could say about anybody on eartl but she took his point.

She was listening intently, wanting to know every detail. She wante to know about the stent they had inserted, but she couldn't escape th noise of the kids who were laughing and playing and shouting.

"The anaesthetist called him *a ticking time bomb.*"

The man had cheated death, and the woman had narrowly escaped personal tragedy of unfathomable proportions. The children were tw four and six years old.

When she collected her husband from the hospital, they high-five each other and hugged. They had been so lucky. They had dodged fatal bullet. They had wrenched the man away from the precipice.

It would have been healthy to take a week off then, to process th trauma; seek counselling. But just because you almost lose you husband, doesn't mean you can stop to think about it. There wa double the work to do while he recovered. Squawking mouths to fee school meetings, cookie sales, headaches. More hospital bills, mo deadlines to meet. More dark nights of thinking about how close the had come. The black water kept rising, and the woman kept treadin She was only just keeping her kids afloat, and now the man had joine them, too.

Some of the stories the woman wrote were disturbing. Sometimes sl chose the story, and sometimes the story chose her. One was about mother who drowns her children. The research was harrowing, an the woman lay awake at night with the sheer heart-rending horror c it. She avoided the story of the lost children for as long as she could, but it demanded to be written.

The work was both the woman's escape and her reason for getting up in the mornings. It was what she was meant to do. Write, publish, repeat. Build an empire that could pay the bills. She needed to keep going, keep reaching. A good writing session energised her and made the world feel right. Her craving to create was deeper than her need to rest. Her phone kept ringing and buzzing; emails pinged; messages vibrated. Everyone wanted to talk, talk, talk. The house maintenance drained her; the kids pecked at her. People said she was such a hard worker, but what they didn't see was the escape it gave her; the energy it afforded her. They didn't see the bedrock inside her that was entirely made up of the words she had written and the words she was yet to write.

But even with the freedom her work gave her, she couldn't get away from the approaching thundercloud that pulsed with imminent danger. As the darkness swirled in, the static notched up. She didn't feel like herself. Nightmares of her baby dying in the ambulance —*Children can be unpredictable*—in the hospital room, in her cot at home. Dreams of her children disappearing or being knocked over by cars. Her husband lying on the bottom of a pool made of glass. Her books turning into small white leech-like worms in her hands.

The eggs were in the paper, the printer in her terror-dream said.

Burn them all, she told him.

He shook his head. *It's too late. Your books are hatching all over the world.*

The woman remembered the movie scene where Juliane Moore's character—a housewife—wants to kill herself. She bakes her son a birthday cake, leaves him with a neighbour, then goes to a hotel room to commit suicide. She lies on the bed and has visions of the room being filled with water. She's on the island in the middle, lying on her back, looking at the ceiling as the water rises. At the last minute, she decides to live. She wrenches her own body off the precipice and escapes to start a new life.

Running away from her family was not an option for the woman; there'd be no point. Her husband and children WERE the point. They were where the rawness was, the joy and pain and anger and love and the relentless tug of life. But it was too much.

I don't know how you do it, people said. *How do you cope?*

I'm not coping, the woman said. *I feel completely overwhelmed all the time.* But that's not what people want to hear.

One night, her husband was working and she—trying to meet a deadline and failing—started cooking dinner late. The children were all talking to her at the same time. Her right eye had been twitching for weeks. The four-year-old climbed onto the counter and accidentally knocked down a bottle of plum sauce, which shattered all over the floor. The baby, barefoot, wouldn't listen when the woman warned her to stay back from the shards of glass. The lump in her throat swelled so much it felt like she couldn't breathe past it; it was a ball of fire she couldn't swallow. She went days and days feeling close to tears; blinking them away, telling herself to pull herself together. The tears were puzzling. She wasn't sad; she had a lucky life. Too lucky.

What is wrong with me? she demanded as she scraped the syrupy sauce off the floor. *Am I going mad?* It was a legitimate question; there was a history of mental illness in her family. She has always had a bright, resilient mind. She thought she was immune.

. . .

The static took over her life when she wasn't looking. Her eyes were open, but her vision was crowded with sticky hands and urgent appeals for everything but rest.

It's just a very demanding time of life, she told herself.

It's not going to get any less demanding, she heard her obstetrician riff.

The woman knew she could run away, but she didn't want to. She could stop working, but stopping writing would just be a different kind of suicide.

I'm not coping, the woman told her husband. It hurt her to admit it. Their friends joked about her invisible superhero cape. It didn't make sense to her. The year before had been the challenging time and she had coped. The six-book contract, the gaping credit card deficit, the late nights, the health scares. The dark water rose and fell and then rose higher than before.

Things were going well. The kids were thriving; the woman's career had notched up.

This year's easier, she kept telling herself. Except that for some reason it wasn't.

She battled to write. She couldn't grasp common words, and her thoughts were being choked by the static. She thought it was a phase and kept trying, but day after day, the anxiety shut down her brain. It became harder to get out of bed in the mornings. Her hair began to break when she brushed it and then began to fall out. Nightmares haunted her. She couldn't tread anymore. She commanded her legs to keep kicking, but they were no longer responding. It's not as dramatic as a snapping tendon. It's a gradual slowing down to a stop, and then, helpless, you begin to sink.

.   .   .

She knew she had to get out of her head but she didn't know how. She postponed some publishing deadlines and took some time off. One day while walking home, the hot stone in her throat began to choke her. Standing on the sidewalk in the shade of the Jacaranda trees she hyperventilated and wept. She wasn't sad. She didn't know where the tears had come from, but she knew it was time to get help.

Three weeks after she had refused the idea of medication, she was in her doctor's office, the number of a cognitive behavioural therapist and a prescription for anti-anxiety drugs clutched in her clammy hands.

You take this one for the anxiety, but it might make you feel more anxious in the beginning. So you take this one, too, just till your body adjusts.

It was a relief to hold the boxes of pills in her hands.

For two nights in a row on the new medication, despite one of them being a sedative, her eyes clicked open at 2 am and her heart and mind raced. During the day, the world looked different. Her hands sweated on the keyboard, her legs swung on their own accord, and she couldn't settle her mind enough to write.

Here's something to help you sleep, said the doctor.

Uh-oh, the woman thought, taking the third prescription on top of the other two. *I know how this story ends. I've seen the movie; I know the tropes. You keep taking more and more till your life implodes.*

But that's not what happened.

As her body adjusted to the drugs, life slowed down and the static faded. The woman began to feel lighter. She began noticing the beautiful trees on their street again; the orange pop of the Autumn leaves swirling around them as they walked to school. She stopped rushing verywhere and felt the breeze on her skin. Her body felt healthier; er hair stopped falling out. She began enjoying her children again, aughing with them and dancing in the kitchen. When she hugged hem, the embrace was no longer tinged with fear. The woman started issing her husband again.

ecent symptoms she hadn't attributed to anxiety began to fade. Her ngers stopped trembling; her memory improved. She could write gain. She realised that swallowing the small white pills every norning wasn't about giving in, it was about protecting her body and er brain. The world was burning, and she loved her children too uch. They were living in an eroded reality and she needed all the rmour she could get.

he dark water started to drain away, and she could finally breathe asily and rest her legs. The thunderclouds that had been crashing owards her retreated. The woman pulled her family closer, and they ood like that, huddled together, as the sun began to burn through the og. The four-year-old told one of his silly knock-knock jokes and they ll laughed, and it felt real and raw and good, and there were no more ears to fight. The hard stone in her throat had melted away.

'm fine, the woman told herself, and she realised it was no longer a lie.

∾

6

SKYREST

A note from the author:

This story is based in the 'When Tomorrow Calls' world and contains minor spoilers.

It's an excerpt I adapted from the book 'What Have We Done' that I believe works as a short story.

If you're planning on reading the futuristic thriller series and want to avoid the minor spoilers in this story,

please email me at janita@firefinchpress.com *and I'll send you the prequel novella as a gift.*

SKYREST

"**Y**ou ready for your first shift, Girdler?"

Lewis stands at Zack's sliding door, muscles flexing; his grey beard is neatly clipped. The bell rings.

"I think so." Zack doesn't mind the idea of hard work today. It might help with his nerves. His mentor gestures for him to follow, and they join the rest of the prisoners as they stream out of the residence and into the adjacent factory. Zack calls it a factory, but to be honest, he still doesn't know what products SkyRest makes. He receives a few mildly interested looks from the others, but most of them ignore him. Soldier ants, worker bees: all in the same grey soft-cotton kit.

"What is the actual work?"

"That's not an easy one to answer," says Lewis.

Zack laughs without humour. "What do you mean?"

"It's not like we're working on an assembly line, right? We're not manufacturing Fong Kong. This isn't bloody Bilchen. It's a crim colony. A penal labour camp."

"But what do we do?"

"They identify what needs doing and they funnel us accordingly."

"But what? What work?"

Why is Lewis being so evasive?

"Anything. Anything that requires labour as long as—"

"Yes?"

"As long as we're not seen."

"By who?"

"By the clients. By the pretty people in the honeycomb. We're like ...

the midnight elves. You know, the little crims who steal inside and do all the work. Like an invisible workforce, you know? The ghost in the machine. No one wants to see the elves. It breaks the spell."

They keep walking.

"So, give me some examples, so that I know what to expect."

Lewis sighs. Zack can see him thinking: *I'm too old for this shit.*

"Okay, so ... the day before yesterday we were chopping wood for the incinerator. The day before that, we were creating seed eggs. Before that: chopping bloody onions. Before that: re-potting saplings. Birch, I think they were. Silver birch."

"What are seed eggs?"

Lewis holds up a hand to stop him from asking more questions.

"You're going to be in here a long time. If you want to be my assigned initiate you're gonna need to learn some patience."

"Sorry," says Zack.

"I'm not mad. I'm just telling you like it is."

They trot into an artificial greenhouse. There are no windows because it's deep underground, but the ceiling is covered in thousands of lo-glo bulbs, and the plants—thousands upon thousands of plants—reach up to their fake suns like disciples who don't yet know they've been swindled.

They line up along the rows of aeroponic vegetation. How many are there of them? Zack does a quick headcount. Two hundred? Each row seems to contain a different plant. Theirs has a purple flower.

"Slow and steady," says Lewis, tapping his lapel. "Slow and steady wins the race."

Zack looks at Lewis's lapel. "Hey. You got another stripe."

Lewis's eyes twinkle. "Close now," he says, "real close. I think you had something to do with it."

"I doubt it," says Zack.

"You filled in the mentee satisfaction report, right?"

"Well, there was a form. It asked how I would rate my initiation experience."

"Right," says Lewis. "I think that's what tipped the scales. I mean, I knew I was close."

"What's the first thing you're going to do?" asks Zack. "You know, when you're up there?"

"I'm gonna go for a swim. Did you see that swimming pool?"

"No," says Zack. "I thought pools were illegal."

"Not in state institutions. Not when they service a community like this."

"You saw it?"

"Oh yeah. Oh man, that pool. As blue as the bloody Atlantic ocean. I haven't been for a swim since 2009."

"That does sound pretty good."

"And then, then ... I'm going to have a meal. A proper meal. And a CinnaCola, with ice. Real ice. Not fake ice."

"I don't think they make that anymore. CinnaCola, I mean."

Lewis looks disappointed.

"Listen up, residents," says a familiar voice from the front of the greenhouse.

A medium close-up of Bernard's toad-skinned face beams into a hexagonal-framed hologram above them. There's a hush.

We're going to be spraying the plants today. It's important that you spray them hard enough to dislodge any insects—"

So they've given her a job to do.

—but not so hard that you damage the leaves or uproot the organism."

Bernard nods at the creep holding the holocam, and they track down to her hands, where she demonstrates the correct procedure. Zack can't help cringing when there's a close-up of her fingers and her broad, flat fingernails. She was in his room again last night. He heard the door slide open, and something inside him shrivelled up like it would never be the same again. And now she's here to stay.

What are these plants, anyway?" he whispers to Lewis.

It's bloody alfalfa," says Lewis. "Can't you tell?"

Once the plants are sprayed and inspected for any malformations or disease, the workers move on to other things. Some go to help in the kitchen, some, the laundry. Zack and Lewis are enlisted to saw and chip wood, along with another ten men. What surprises Zack most is how much space there is down here. The outside building—that white honeycomb shard planted into the earth—is the tip of an iceberg. An anthill that is rooted deeply and widely under the surface.

Be careful," warns Lewis, looking at the humming machine. "These are industrial chippers. They'll chew your arm off if you daydream."

They start feeding the appliance with the hunks of wood. It makes short work of even the hardest wedges of timber. They both grunt and sweat with the effort of hauling the heavy pieces.

No offence, but ... aren't you too old for this kind of work?" Zack is only half joking.

Sod off," says Lewis. They both know he is the stronger of the two.

It's gratifying labour, and the air fills with a dusty forest fragrance tha penetrates their paper masks. They bag all the wood chips and pac them into trolley cages which are wheeled away by another team They sweep the floor till it's spotless; so that no one would be able t say there were twelve men in here making whole trees disappear.

After an exhausting eight hours, the bell rings, and they stroll back t their residence, stretching sore muscles and rubbing dirt off their skin Bernard follows them from behind. Zack ruffles his hair and sawdus falls onto his shoulders, and his cuff beeps green.

"Hey," says Lewis. "The gods approve!"

Zack frowns at him, and Lewis slaps him on the back.

"You got your first credit. You get a Reward! What are you going t choose?"

"I don't know."

"You don't know?" Lewis wipes his arms and hands with a damp rag.

"I guess I'll look through the catalogue."

"You need to set up your wishlist, man. Most of us have lists a mil long. You don't even have an idea?"

Zack still doesn't have an appetite, and there's nothing he's seen i Lewis's room that he wants to replicate, but then he gets it.

"A book," says Zack. It's exactly what his atrophying brain require "I'll request a book."

Lewis shakes his head. "Sorry, man. Down here? No books allowed."

The next day, Zack and the other SkyRest prisoners are led into th hall to work. They are given special protective gear. Thin plastic ove alls that crunch when you walk, wide face masks, and biolatex gloves. Even though they are still deep underground, the air is less stale than usual.

The prison guard with grey hair and a voice like dusk stands in front of them. His name is Xoli. The younger guard—a blond, fresh-faced assistant—films him so that his face is broadcast in the hexagonal holoframe above the residents.

"Good morning," he says, and the men mutter their replies. "You'll be wondering why you've been given extra kit. It's because we're dealing with a new substance today. It's part of our experimentation in a new, cutting-edge technology, and we need your help. It's not without risk, though, so please be careful and keep your prophylactix on at all times."

There's a murmur of interest. Virgin tasks down here are few and far between, so getting to do new work seems like something to look forward to. The men are instructed to move towards the trestle tables, and the day leaders peel away the covers to reveal large tubs of dark brown organic matter.

"Now for those of you with foraging experience," says Xoli, and there are a few laughs, "You'll know that this—" He holds up a large lily-shaped, charcoal-coloured mushroom. "—is called a Black Trumpet. Cornucopioides. Also known as black chanterelle, and ... Trumpet of Death."

Zack studies the tub in front of him. He can see the fungi between the humus and decayed leaves.

"Now, mycologists would usually tell you that there's nothing to fear from a black chanterelle, and they'd be right. In fact, these mush-rooms, in the wild, are really quite delicious and will do you no harm."

Xoli holds up his specimen, and the camera zooms in.

"However, this batch of fungi has been adapted by our bioburial scientists, who spliced its helix with Dermestid."

The room is quiet.

"Anyone?"

A few frowns and head-shakes.

"Derme-stid. Skin Beetle. A Dermestid is a flesh-eating beetle."

Zack's skin crawls with imaginary insect legs.

"So, I introduce to you ... *Carnacraterellus cornucopioides*."

"A man-eating mushroom," says Zack.

Xoli looks pleased. "Correct."

The men murmur. Xoli talks them through the process: find the mushrooms, identify the mycelia, harvest the spores, store them safely in the envelopes or soil trays provided.

"Please work carefully," he says. "And, whatever you do, don't breathe the spores in. As you can imagine, you don't want these suckers seeding your lungs."

Later, in his room, Zack lies on his mat and swipes through the SkyRest Reward Catalogue. What he really wants now is sleeping pills, but those are contraband, too. He hasn't had a good night's sleep since his arrest. Although, even if he had the pills, he probably wouldn't take them. Only one thing is worse than Bernard watching him sleep, and that's not even knowing she's watching him sleep.

He might request a bed or a decent mattress at least, but those cost a lot more than the one credit he has. He'd have to save up if he wants a big purchase like that. He sees a small mirror advertised. Perhaps he should get that for above the sink? He doesn't know what he looks like anymore. Maybe it's best to keep it that way. Prison pyjamas and artificial light, shrinking brain. Thinking about looking at himself every day in these conditions make him decide against it. He imagines himself as hollow-eyed and hollow-boned. That's what it feels like, anyway.

He scrolls and scrolls until he eventually finds something to buy. The app congratulates him on his redemption (if only it were that easy) and informs him to expect delivery in the next open chute.

The dinner bell rings, and Zack joins Lewis's table in the cafeteria. Lewis points at him and says, "New guy. Girdler," for the benefit of the other prisoners. The men shoot him cursory glances. One or two mumble *hi*.

"You're not eating?" asks Lewis.

Zack shakes his head. "Not hungry."

"You gotta eat."

"What is it?" asks Zack.

"Who bloody knows," says Lewis, and some of the other men laugh.

Zack grabs a tray and chooses the least unattractive option at the counter. Some kind of tofurkey with grey sauce and matching mash. Some fresh green and purple leaves on the side that makes the food look slightly less dire.

Back at the table, he takes a bite of mashed potato. Or, at least, he thinks it's mashed potato. It's difficult to swallow.

"You'll get used to it," says Lewis.

"I doubt it," Zack replies.

"Soon *you'll* be eating decent food," says a shiny-scalped man to Lewis. He wiggles his eyebrows at the colourful stripes on Lewis's lapel and points his fork up to the ceiling, smiling. There is grey mash in his teeth.

"Ah," says Lewis, clearly relishing the thought. He'd been working down here a long, long time and was so close to earning his release.

"I heard they've got an artisanal ice cream shop up there," says a man who looks like a professional wrestler. "There are, like, a hundred different flavours. And if they don't have the flavour you want, you can make a request, and they'll make it for you."

"Ah," repeats Lewis.

"I'd ask for salted butterscotch," says the wrestler. "In a sugar cone."

"Black Choxolate," says the bald man, but there's not much hope in his voice. He only has two stages on his lapel.

"Eighties Bubblegum," says Lewis. "Remember that? Summers at the South Coast. Blue ice-cream dripping down your chin."

For a moment they all look lost in their memories of childhood treats and open skies.

"And you'll forget all about us," says baldy.

"I bloody won't," says Lewis.

"Yes, you will," says the wrestler. "And you should."

～

"I'm ready," says Zack to Lewis as they finish their game of table tennis.

"Hmm?"

Lewis is buoyed by the dinner conversation about his inevitable elevaon, and Zack wants to take advantage of his good mood. "You said ou'd tell me what SkyRest does when I was ready."

ewis scoffs. "You're not ready. You've barely been here five minutes."

Lewis. Please."

Ie puts his bat down and takes a long, hard look at Zack. The ball brates on the table, then comes to a stop. Eventually, Lewis capitu-tes with a shrug.

ewis and Zack enter the small dim cineroom, and Lewis dials up the ghts, interrupting the prisoners watching an old nature documentary.

Hey!" some of them say, before realising who it is.

Sorry to interrupt, gents," Lewis says, pausing the film. "We need the oom."

he men complain under their breath, but no one dares confront ewis. They stand up and stroll out.

ack flips through the available titles on DVD. The titles are milque-oast. No new releases, no sex or violence. Just old wildlife shows, lean sitcoms, and vintage feel-good films. He picks one out, cracks pen the cover and inspects it. 'Eternal Sunshine of the Spotless lind'.

ewis laughs at the old tech. "When's the last time you saw one of hose?"

ven the dusty DVD player looks a hundred years old.

ewis changes the amp source then types in a code to unlock a kyRest-branded video. When prompted to confirm, he looks at Zack. You sure you want to know this shit?"

ack nods.

"It's like bad porn," he says.

"What?"

"I mean, it's not X-rated. But, like bad porn, it's not something yo can't un-see."

Zack nods again, and Lewis purses his lips and clicks play.

They grab a seat in the front row, and the film begins. The initial sh is drone-footage of the architecture that rises a mile above them: fla tering angles of the white honeycomb shard among the deep green the surrounding forest, and a woman's honey-tongued voice-ov begins.

"Welcome," she says, "to SkyRest."

The voice sounds like Gaelyn's, the attractive woman who had ove seen his admission and appointed Lewis as his babysitter.

An ultra-realistic animation of a tree falling in a forest occurs. The tr soon greys and shrinks as it breaks down, and new growth—brigl green saplings—shoots up from the nurse log.

"It's easy to become disconnected from nature when you're living high-speed urban life," says the calming voice. "Part of this disco nect is thinking of death as an inherently negative experience. B what makes SkyRest different from other urban vertic cemeteries?"

Unseen things click into place one after another in Zack's mind, li someone shuffling a deck of cards.

"SkyRest offers clients a variety of burial options—"

Hexagonal frames appear on the screen to illustrate the available alte natives, and the first frame is enlarged: Inside is a tombstone.

"Our traditional burial contains all the hallmarks of a convention burial, except that it takes place on one of our sky storeys. You a welcome to visit the resting place of your loved one any time of day or night."

The next frame is an urn on a mantelpiece. "If you end up selecting customary cremation, we have a variety of options to deal with the ashes. These include, amongst others: having them mixed with oil paint, and commissioning an artist to create a unique work for you. Having them distilled and turned into jewellery, or having them buried under the rootball of a sapling that you can take home and plant in your garden."

Seems sensible. So far, Zack doesn't see what the big deal is.

"If you don't want to keep the remains, we also offer water cremation."

Okay, that's a new one, but still ... hardly controversial.

"These are all popular burial solutions," says the speaker, "but none of them are environmentally friendly, and at SkyRest we strive for a carbon-double-negative footprint. If it's also important to you to leave the world causing minimal damage, you may consider our earth-friendly options."

Zack's ears prick up; the SkyRest logo animates on screen.

"SkyRest introduces ... Recomposition™. Your Doorway to Immortality."

Immediately Zack thinks of zombies. Does this place bring dead bodies back to life? A shameful amount of bank has been spent on immortality tech, but as he thinks it, he knows this isn't that kind of place. Everything he's seen has been deep green and eco-devoted—and he's petty sure zombies don't fit into that equation.

"For most people, the suddenness and permanence of death is difficult to accept, especially when it's a loved one. With SkyRest's trade-marked Recomposition™ technology, your spirit can live on by nurturing the earth that sustained you during your lifetime."

Zack hardly blinks.

"Traditional burials are anything but natural. Bodies are preserved with the known carcinogen, formaldehyde, and then sealed in caskets that further embalm them, taking up valuable land and leaching poison into the ground. Even cremations are not without environmental damage: a single cremation pumps a toxic cocktail of chemicals into the air. In fact, our legal team here at SkyRest predicts that both of these options will be banned by 2040. Recomposition™ offers a positive solution to those looking for an earth-friendly burial."

The animation of the nurse log returns.

"Recomposition™ interlaces the cycles of life into the meaning-hungry, time-starved urban fabric and reminds us that, as humans, we're deeply connected to the natural ebb and flow of Mother Earth."

A young woman is lying on a forest floor, asleep. Dead? Naked, apart from some strategically placed autumn leaves. Her long blonde hair is styled against the dark ground. More and more fallen leaves cover her pale skin until she is no longer visible. The earth has swallowed her up.

"There you go." Lewis pauses the video. "Happy now?"

"Yes," says Zack. "No. I don't understand what the big deal is. Why the secrecy?"

"What can I say? It's death. People get cagey."

"How does it work?"

"You want me to draw you a bloody picture?"

"Can we watch to the end?" Zack already knows the answer and is frustrated. He kicks the cabinet of DVDs. He just wants answers. Is it too much to ask?

Lewis turns off the screen. "You're not ready for the end."

"I'm sorry about last night," says Zack to Lewis over breakfast. Lewis raises his white eyebrows at him and motions for him to sit.

"No worries. I expected it. It's always difficult for initiates to process the work they do here." Lewis pushes his plate away. Zack sits and looks at the abandoned food. No-egg omelette? Dutch baby pancake? He can't stand the idea of eating food he can't identify.

"No one's perfect, right? We've all done wrong. Inside of here and out."

"Right."

"But there is one thing." Lewis traces a scar on the table. "And I don't mean to offend."

Zack looks at him.

"Have you looked in the mirror, lately?"

"What?"

"You look like shit, man."

Zack finger-combs his hair, rubs his eyes. "I haven't been sleeping."

"I can see that. Your eyes have more baggage than a supermodel."

"I actually think I feel worse than I look."

"Not possible," says Lewis, and throws his head back, laughing. A few residents stop eating their omelette/pancake to look at him, and Zack laughs too.

"Any advice?" he asks.

"Advice? Sure. Get a bloody mirror."

Zack laughs. "Funnily enough, I did consider it. But being down here is torturous enough without having to look at my own reflection every morning."

"No, seriously," says Lewis. "You'd better start sleeping. And start eating! The way you're looking, well..." He gestures at the building above them. "If you're not careful, they'll be using you in their next video."

The now-familiar siren sounds, letting them know that their work shift is beginning. The men sigh, bin what's left on their plates, and lope out of the cafeteria. This time they're led to a hall Zack has not yet seen. A warden shows them how to re-pot plants that have grown out of their containers. Roses, hydrangeas, maples, trailing Boston ivy, Virginia creeper. Considering yesterday's video, he reckons taking a thriving Boston ivy plant home instead of ashes is a good thing. You could have this urn of ashes in your house that you don't know what to do with, or you could have this plant that can cover a whole wall—a whole building—and flicker from season to season between green and red. A daily reminder that the person you've lost is not really lost at all. Or a rose bush: the blooms of your beloved.

They tap the plants' containers to release the roots, then ease them into the soft new soil. It's therapeutic work, and Zack starts relaxing for the first time since being here. They play classical music over the sound system. His shoulders unknot; his brain untangles. After the re-potting, they have to shift some soil in wheelbarrows, then they're instructed to sweep up and bag the sawdust and kindling in the wood-chipping room. The exercise feels good. The work is easy and monotonous and becomes like meditation. He keeps checking his cuff for his next Reward, and wonders how long it will be till he gets the first stripe on his lapel.

This place isn't so bad. Then he corrects himself: *It could be worse.*

After they've showered, and they're waiting for dinner, they hang out

Lewis's room. Lewis is still in good spirits, doing arm-lifts and eating protein pretzels. His bare chest ripples with muscles a man half his age would be proud to have, and his tattoo seems darker than usual, the colours richer. The illustration seems to pulse on his skin, as if the dragon is alive.

"Getting ready for that swim?" Zack asks.

"I can taste that water, you know. I can feel it streaming through my hair in that first dive. Cooling my scalp."

"Going to be a good feeling," says Zack. "After all this time."

"Oh, yes." He drops from the bar then downs half a bottle of water. "Oh, yes."

Lewis offers him the SkyRest-branded packet of pretzels. Zack hesitates.

"Go on," says Lewis. "They're not going to bite you."

Zack reaches his hand inside the bag, grabs a few then sprinkles them in his other palm. Tentatively puts one in his mouth. It's not too bad.

"Will you tell me the rest of it?" asks Zack.

"The rest of what?"

"The rest of the video. Tell me how they do it?"

"All right," he says, sitting down. "Sure. Why the hell not?"

Zack eats another pretzel. They're quite good, actually.

"What do you want to know?"

"Everything."

"Ever heard of Ouroboros?" asks Lewis.

"Your tattoo," says Zack. "The serpent that devours its own tail."

Zack knows the ancient Egyptian circular symbol of eternal retur
that has been re-used and recycled by philosophical trains from Gree
magic to alchemy to Kundalini health goths.

"Right. So they have this system going here. It's completely sel
sustaining. Everything you eat, wear, or touch in this place comes fro
this place. *It is its own* immortality."

"Recomposition."

"Recomp's the main technology, yes. There are others on the men
and even more that they're experimenting with."

"How does the recomp work?"

"Recomp is when they take the ... nitrogen-rich material—"

"The what?"

"The nitrogen-rich material. That's what they call it."

"Do you mean, the bodies? The dead bodies?"

"Yes, that's what it means."

"So they take the nitrogen-rich—the bodies—and place them inside
mound of carbon-rich material ... so that's the sawdust, and the woo
chips. They add a bit of moisture, some extra nitro on top to get
going. Maybe some alfalfa."

Zack remembers the pretty purple alfalfa blooms they had worked o
during a previous shift. The alfalfa on his plate yesterday. What ha
Lewis said about them? That they're a feminine herb, an element o
the earth, and especially good on sandwiches.

"Then the microbes do their thing. The microbial activity gets the pi
cooking. Their heat kills the bad shit. The pathogens. That's what yo
can feel."

"What do you mean?"

"We call it our underfloor heating. The warmth, from the middle of the building? That's the core. That's where it all happens. Bodies in the top. Compost out the bottom."

Human compost.

Saliva rushes into Zack's mouth. He tries to swallow his revulsion.

"Then they cure the compost. Sometimes the clients want to take the compost home. They plant a tree or whatever. Or they let someone here do it for them. They plant one of those saplings in the forest at the back. Put a tag on the tree, or a bench with a silver plaque underneath it. But most of the compost goes unclaimed. That's the stuff we use for the aeroponics. It's what we use to grow everything in here."

Zack spits out the pretzel.

Lewis laughs. "Ja, that's pretty much the standard reaction."

Zack looks around the room. His uniform, the linen, Lewis's snax, the soap, the toothpaste, all emblazoned with the SkyRest logo.

"Yes," says Lewis. "Even the toiletries. Hemp oil and Miswak and Homosapien. So best get used to it."

Zack reaches for his water and rinses his mouth out, spits the water into Lewis's basin.

"Once you've had time to process it, you'll see that it makes complete sense. It's the full circle, you know? None of that embalming shit. No poisoning the well. None of that hanging onto dead bodies. If you think about it, being attached to a dead body is way weirder than letting it go back to the earth, you know? No waste, no harm, just energy doing its thing. Going round and round as it should. The process is a beautiful thing."

"Does everyone in here ... Do the rest of the prisoners know?"

"Most of them. Some have been red-flagged. Admin decided it's best not to tell them. The truth doesn't serve everybody."

Zack feels ill.

The bell rings for dinner time.

Zack is in the forest. Dark as dread. He's running from something. Someone? The leaves hit his face, the thin black branches whipping his cheeks and arms as he races away from the danger. Where is he? This must be the forest that surrounds the crim colony. Has he escaped? He runs despite the dark, despite not being able to see more than a metre in front of him, despite the soft mounds of earth that threaten to swallow his feet and twist his ankles. He runs and runs despite not having any energy left in his limbs. Panic pushes him forward; makes his legs feel weightless.

He's wearing his suit and tie; he doesn't know how. He doesn't know in which direction he's running. He'll keep going until he reaches the edge then strategise when he gets there. He needs to leave the threat behind.

But there's a problem with his plan or, rather, a problem with the forest. Because he keeps running, but he's not getting anywhere. He can sense that despite his frantic pace, he hasn't moved an inch—an enchanted forest, a cursed forest. All of a sudden, he's flying through the air and lands in a shallow ditch full of leaves. The air is knocked out of him. He touches the soil on the banks that surround him and understands it's not a ditch at all. It's way too deep. It's a rectangular hole, six feet down. A grave. The realisation doesn't help to get the oxygen he needs into his lungs. The air is thick with the aroma of humus and clay. Leaf mould. Too thick to breathe. He scrabbles to climb out of the hole; he can't find a foothold.

He makes it halfway up the bank of soil when a rock gives way, and he falls back down. He collapses hard, onto his back, and the shock of it keeps him lying like that until his head stops buzzing. But in the place of the buzzing is another sound: a whispering, rustling, an animal ticking, hundreds of insect legs. There's a pinprick on his ankle, then on his hand. He jumps up and shakes off the things. One is trying to get inside his ear, and he swipes at it with a yell. Another sharp pain, on his leg, and then there are stings all over as the beetles swarm over him. Zack screams as he tries to sweep them off. As if sensing his panic, they bite down. They want to get their feed before their dinner disappears. He starts to feel the wetness of the trails of blood mixing together. His fingers frantically scrape at the walls of black soil, and one of his nails tears off. Eventually, he finds a root to grab onto and uses all the strength the adrenaline gives him to haul himself up and out of the death cube.

Zack pulls off what's left of the flesh-eating beetles and crunches them underfoot. He's dripping blood. Once he's sure he's free of the bugs, he puts his hands on his knees and waits for his lungs to catch up with him. The danger is still present, some unseen evil in the forest, but there's also the danger of him passing out and then there'll be no way he gets out of here alive. How did he get here? All he can remember is—

There's a sound behind him, a dead branch snapping. He spins around, his heart already trying to judder out of his body. Zack tries to make out what—who?—made the noise. He starts reversing and backs into a wide tree trunk. He puts his hands out to steady himself against the bark, but as his palms touch it, he recoils. It doesn't feel right. He turns towards it and yells in fright. Bits of bone are embedded in the bark. Bone bark. The branches further up are cartilage and sinew. There is some hair, some cheekbone. Teeth. Fragments of the pale woman from the video are part of this tree. An eyeball swivels to look at him, and he yells again, wants to run, but his horror keeps him rooted to the spot. A shaft of moonlight casts the softest light on the tree, and Zack realises it's not the woman from the video. It's him.

Zack is yelling into the dark. A large hand is covering his mouth. Spongey, cold skin over his fevered jaw. His eyes click open. It's Bernard trying to suffocate him. He tries to fight her but she has the advantage of being above him and uses all her heft to pin him down, knee on shoulder. He struggles and struggles, but is made weak by the starvation, the sleep-dep, the forest nightmare. Zack tries to call for Lewis, but her hand cancels out any trace of his voice. Gradually he stops struggling, thinking she will kill him now, she'll kill him and would that be that bad? But as he stops fighting her, she eases off too, until there is just one soft hand on his mouth; the other goes to her own, an index finger crosses her lips telling him to be quiet.

"Shhh," Bernard says.

The day's chute delivery arrives with a neatly wrapped Rewards parcel for Zack. The bald resident—Spud, they call him—hands it over.

"Congratulations!" Spud says, slapping Zack on the shoulder. Zack thinks he means for the Reward, but then he looks down at what Spud is eyeing: he has a colour stripe on his lapel. His first Stage.

Zack swings by Lewis's room and is shocked when it's empty—not only of Lewis but also all his things. It's completely stripped down to the basics, with just a sleeping mat on the floor.

"Isn't it great?" says a voice in his ear.

Zack spins around, holding his Reward parcel against his chest. It was meant to be a gift for Lewis. Spud is grinning.

Zack's mind is furry with last night's events. "What?"

Isn't it great?" Spud says again. "He's gone! Promoted!"

Jack shakes his head. Of course. Lewis has been Elevated. That's good news. That's excellent news, but why does it make his stomach simmer with dread? He looks down at the gift. His nails are lined with dirt, and one of his fingernails is torn. He blinks, and the soil disappears, and his nail is no longer torn. He feels as if he is losing his grip on reality.

There is a jovial atmosphere in the cafeteria at breakfast time. Word has spread that Lewis has finally been elevated and the other residents are exuberant. Part of it is for Lewis, and part is the stoking of their hopes that they, too, will one day be promoted upstairs. Two men at an adjacent table each have only one more Stage to go. They laugh over their salty French toast at the inmates who joke around them about the bright blue pool and the craft ice cream and the all-you-can-watch film suites.

Jack's stomach is still roiling when it's time to start the work shift. He's left Lewis's gift in his room—still wrapped—even though he's sure he'll never see him again. They walk over to a hall where trestle tables are set out with old-school sewing machines, and the men are divided into those who can sew and those who can't. Zack is in the latter group, so he is tasked with unrolling and cutting fabric according to overhead projector templates. They set to work as the machines hum in the background. Usually, the white noise would be calming, but today it's as if the buzzing is inside his head. His new shift-partner is a slimy man with nervous eyes and adds to Zack's feeling of unease.

After two hours of work, a bell rings, and the men sigh and stretch their arms and backs before they're shepherded to the next task. Zack trails behind the group, trying to avoid his new partner. There will be a five-minute toilet break before the next grind begins. Without really thinking, without even meaning to, Zack peels off from the crowd and slips into a dark room. He knows they're monitored continuously-knows they're watching his every move—so he doesn't understand why he's doing it. If he gets caught, he'll get docked any Rewards due to him. He may even get stripped of his first Stage. But there is an instinct stronger than fear, stronger than the desire to climb the ladder that leads him away from the others.

Zack slips in quietly and waits for his eyes to adjust to the low light. The space has an earthy smell—is it one of the potting rooms?—but he doesn't see any plants or soil. He blinks, trying to make out what it is in front of him. He inches forward, towards a large dark shape. When he's closer, he sees it's a dozen make-shift platforms built from old building palettes, and they each hold up a large burlap bag with hand-sewn, re-purposed zips.

Wood chips? Sawdust?

But the shape of the bag is wrong. It's too long. It's horizontal. That and the zip makes it look like a—

He moves towards the bag closest to him. As he touches it, the bell rings for the next shift to start, and he jolts. Time to go, but he stays there, his body and brain frozen.

They'll miss him soon; he'll be in trouble. His hand travels back to the zip. The smell is stronger now, the dark humus scent reminding him of his nightmare last night. Damp soil and something else. What is it? He pulls the handle of the zip down.

Inside the bag is more brown burlap, wrapped around a sphere, like dressing. Zack keeps unzipping the rest of it and flinches when he sees that the round bandaged thing is attached to a neck, and a torso. There's a noise in his ears, a humming. It's the adrenaline telling him to run.

So it's a dead body. So what? It's to be expected, isn't it, in a place like this?

The body is ivory, veined with blue. Zack zips it up again. He needs to go. They've probably noticed he's missing. If he goes now, he can still use the excuse of an extended toilet break or—less convincingly—that he got lost. If he doesn't get back now, there'll be someone in here to drag him away. He moves to the next bag and opens it. An ash marble torso, waiting to be recycled. One more, he tells himself, he doesn't know why. The Net knows he doesn't want to see another one of these cold-butter bodies. But the next body isn't pale. The skin of the muscular neck is loam-coloured and wrinkled, and as the zip moves, tooth by tooth, opening the bag, something in Zack knows what's inside before his brain clicks. He sees the top of the tattoo that he knows so well: Ouroboros.

It's Lewis. It's Lewis.

Lewis, who is supposed to be ten storeys above him, swimming laps in a crystal pool.

Zack stares at the rest of the tattoo: the dragon's head, its circular body, eating its own tail. He draws away, realises he's close to hyperventilating. Then he opens the bag further, and there's a steady ribbon of that soil smell—and now Zack identifies it—mushrooms. Forest mushrooms. And he sees openings in Lewis's skin—his stomach and thighs —like a sea-sponge, dark holes stretched by and embroidered with thriving mushrooms where they have rolled spikes over his skin and sprinkled in the shroomspores of the fungi that is eating his flesh. Dark meat with mushroom gills.

Zack turns his head away from the body bag and sprays vomit onto the black concrete floor. Water and bile splash out of him. He wants to run, but his body heaves and heaves. When he straightens up, there is a silhouette at the door.

Two guards come running, almost falling over Bernard in their hurry to get to Zack. They stumble and shine their powerful flashlights into his eyes.

"Don't do anything stupid," she says.

It's a bit late for that.

The guards—Xoli and Samuel—move forward and Zack puts his arms up in surrender, wonders distractedly why they didn't just drop him with a current from the cuff. In his blinded state he has a flashback of Lewis's myco-ravaged flesh and almost vomits again. He covers his mouth with the back of his hand. There are arms around him as the men guide him away from Lewis and the other body bags in the room.

"Where to?" asks Samuel.

"Solitary, for now," says Xoli. "Till they tell us otherwise."

What had Lewis said about solitary confinement? To avoid it at all costs. You go in the Cooler, you'll never be the same. That's if you're lucky enough to come out. Lewis said that 'luck' and 'solitary' do not often go hand in hand. Zack's head is spinning. He can't get around the fact that Lewis is dead.

The young guard blinks. He seems surprised at the harshness of the punishment, but sets his jaw and moves Zack along.

"Stop," says Bernard, as they get to the door. "I'll deal with him." She looks smug. A cat that finally has the canary in her claws.

"But—"

"Girdler has been a menace from the start. There's only one way to deal with him, and I know how." She runs her fingers up and down her baton, moistens her lips.

The guards look uncertain but hand him over anyway. She pushes Zack in front of her.

"Start walking, Prisoner," she says. "The Cooler's got nothing on me."

Zack expects to be taken somewhere dark and beaten to within an inch his life, so when he figures out where they're going, he slows down and waits for his brain to catch up. Bernard pushes him forward.

"Stop dawdling, Prisoner."

His mind is a spiderweb of questions and pictures that won't fade. Bernard grabs two chairs from the common room and marches him to his room; makes him sit in one and takes the other for herself. The residence is empty. Everyone else is still working. He should be used to her observance by now, but can still feel her ugly dishwater eyes washing all over him. Should he be grateful that she saved him from solcon? Or does she have something worse planned?

Heeled footsteps approach. Gaelyn. She arrives and beams at Zack.

"Mister Girdler!" she says, as if they're meeting by coincidence somewhere light and sunny—on a cruise ship, maybe, Cinnacola cocktails in hand—instead of in an underground penal colony cell.

"I do hope you're settling in nicely?"

Zack blinks at her.

"I heard we had an incident," Gaelyn says, but Zack doesn't answer. "Now, I don't want you to worry too much about that. It's natural that you are curious as to how SkyRest functions. I only wish that you had come to me instead of exploring on your own."

"I was just—"

"I know, I know. There's no need to explain yourself." She squeezes his arm. The contact, the human touch, is a surge of warmth. "Now, I see that we need to start taking better care of you."

Bernard snorts.

"You're half the size you were when you arrived a week ago. Is anything the matter?"

What a strange question to ask.

"Tell me what I can do to help you," says Gaelyn. "It's my job to take care of you."

He finds himself gradually defrosting. "I've been ... battling to eat."

"I can see that!" Gaelyn says. "Your cuff is reporting very low blood sugar. Don't worry, I know just the thing." She makes a note on her Tile. "We'll have you sorted out in no time. I don't want you to worry about anything. Are we all okay?"

She searches his face for agreement. Zack wants to agree; he wants to stay on her good side.

"What happened to Lewis?" he asks.

Gaelyn's eyes flicker for a moment, then return to their friendly shine. Her smile is wide. "Oh, we're so thrilled to have him upstairs with us!"

Zack frowns at her.

"If anyone deserved a promotion, it was Lewis! Always such a pleasure to have around. And the way he embraced our philosophy, well, we couldn't be happier to have him with us. We hope that, after this hiccup, you'll work hard to join us too."

"But he's not up there," says Zack, and Bernard's eyes flare.

Shut up, she's saying. *Shut the hell up, Prisoner.*

"What do you mean?"

"Lewis isn't upstairs. He's in a body bag."

Gaelyn looks shocked. "What?"

"Lewis wasn't elevated. He's dead. You can deny it as much as you want, but I saw his dead body in that room."

No wonder you're not yourself! If you think you saw Lewis's body you must have had quite a shock."

I know what I saw."

She frowns again, and feigned worry pouts her lips. "Hmm. This is unfortunate. Maybe the others were right."

What do you mean, the others?"

The Residents' Care Team. Your history during the trial. They predicted you'd need some pharmaceutical assistance."

I don't."

Gaelyn makes another note on her Tile.

Just for a while, until you adjust. Moving here can be a traumatic experience! We need you to be able to cope with your new environment. We can't have people making waves, upsetting the others."

Maybe the others need upsetting," whispers Zack.

Excuse me?" says Gaelyn.

Bernard stomps on his foot. *Shut up!*

Zack raises his voice. "I said maybe the other residents need upsetting."

If I were you," says Gaelyn, "I'd be cautious of what you say next."

Zack wants to shout at her, yell in their faces. He holds himself back. Getting thrown in solitary isn't going to help his cause.

I'm going to let you off with a friendly warning. You can even keep your first Stage. I think you'll find that life is a lot easier down here if you co-operate. The medical team will be here shortly to administer your pharmaceutical treatment."

Maybe I am going mad, Zack thinks. *I've been under a lot of strain.*

Those dreams. The torn fingernail. Maybe I imagined the cold butte
bodies and the man-eating mushrooms.

Gaelyn tucks her Tile into her utility harness and turns to leave.

"What's the first thing he did?" says Zack to her retreating back.

She turns around. "Excuse me?"

"What's the first thing Lewis did when he got up there?"

Gaelyn turns on her most winning smile. "He stripped off the new
clothes we gave him and jumped in the pool!"

7

STAY THE NIGHT

T his story was first written as a play and flighted by South
Africa's national broadcaster, the SABC.

∽

They pulled up to the old, derelict house.

"Well," said Andrew. "I see she hasn't done any maintenance since we
were last here."

"She's a ninety-four-year-old widow," replied Linda. "What did you
expect?"

"You're right. I feel bad, now."

Linda stretched her back. It was aching with the extra weight of her
growing belly. Sometimes she wished she could just take it off for an
hour and hang it on the back of a door, to give her back a break and to
feel light again. "*You* feel bad? Why?"

Andrew pushed his sunglasses up the bridge of his nose and shrugged.
"I could have come over, every now and then. Fixed a few things."

Linda shrugged. "It's not like she lives up the road. It's a two-hour drive. Besides, what you know about DIY is scary."

She wouldn't mention the nursery at home, and how far behind they were in getting the furniture in and painting the place. They didn't even have a crib yet. It made her nervous just thinking about it.

"I could have boarded up those broken windows, for one. Could have hired someone to get rid of that mound of rusty rubbish. Pulled up some blackjacks. A two-hour drive isn't the end of the world."

"There's the drive back home, invariably in the dark. Not safe."

"She has plenty of space. We could have just stayed over."

Linda shook her head. "No. Not allowed. Against the rules."

"What do you mean?" Andrew took off his glasses and frowned at her. "Hodgey was always begging us to stay the night. I've never understood—"

Linda drummed her fingers on her knees. "It's just a thing, okay? An agreement."

Andrew's furrows deepened. "Between you and Hodge?"

"Between Peter and I. We sibling-swore."

"'*Sibling-swore*'? What are you two? Twelve?"

Linda stopped drumming. "We were sixteen, if you must know."

Andrew laughed. "Why? Is the house haunted?"

"In a way."

He stopped laughing, perhaps remembering that Linda had lost her parents when she was sixteen. "In a way?"

"Bad things happen. If you stay over."

. . .

Linda opened her door and levered her aching body out of the vehicle. She walked over to the dead potted plant on the front verandah and retrieved the key from underneath the dusty saucer. After unlocking the stubborn door, she pushed it open, and they both took a quick step backwards.

"God," gasped Andrew, covering his nose. "What is that *smell?*"

Linda had only recently recovered from her "morning" sickness that had lasted all day for six months. The reek made her spin to face the splintering balcony and retch into the field of weeds below. Andrew tried to help her, but she held her hand out to stop him. After so many months of holding her hair back while she vomited she was sure he'd never want to kiss her again. Best he keeps his distance and pass her the bottle of water from the car, both of which he did, without her asking. She wiped her lips with a tissue from her pocket and swirled some water in her mouth.

"Rotting food, probably. It's not like she had time to tidy the fridge before the ambulance picked her up."

"You're telling me," said Andrew. "Look at this pile of old newspapers. Looks like she hasn't had time to tidy the house since 1979." He seemed amused, and in good spirits despite the awful stink. He leaned over to study some of the old headlines. "Who keeps decades-old newspapers?"

"Journalists. Hoarders. And ninety-four-year-old widows who want to hang onto memories."

They took a few tentative steps inside, and Linda opened the curtains and the windows. Dust glittered in the air, and she sneezed. It was far worse than they had expected. You couldn't see the walls for the piles of junk that hid them.

"I'll call someone," said Andrew. "I mean, someone we can hire a skip from. And some extra hands."

"A rubbish skip? We can't just throw her things away, she'll go postal! And we can't have strangers in here. She's very protective of her things."

"We don't have a choice," said Andrew. "This place will take months to sort out, and we've got a weekend. You can't expose yourself to the mould in here, and I've got a bad back."

Linda nodded but felt sad for Granny Hodge. She'd be heartbroken. She was very attached to the ramshackle house.

"Honestly," said Andrew, looking around with a slightly wrinkled up nose. "I'd prefer to burn the whole thing to the ground."

"It would be quicker," said Linda.

"Cheaper," added Andrew.

"And it would probably smell better, too."

∿

"I've got a couple of things for her," said Linda, walking down the creaking stairs with a small tote bag over her arm and holding something stick-like in her hand. She shows it to Andrew. "It's her hundred-year-old toothbrush."

"It looks like it's been used to scrub an entire prison block's toilets."

"Do you think it's worth taking? Or shall I just buy a new one at the hospital? Knowing her, she might want this particular one. Some shampoo, some lotion. Underwear. Do you think two nightgowns is enough? I don't know what old people need."

"Well, don't ask me! Shall we go?"

"Let's have a cup of tea, first."

"We can have a cup of tea at the hospital, with Hodgey."

Linda looked a little pale. "I'd like one now."

"Why are you stalling?"

"I'm not. I'd just really like a cup of tea."

Andrew pursed his lips. He wasn't used to his wife insisting on satisfying any cravings, despite the difficult pregnancy. "Okay. Why don't you put your feet up, and I'll put the kettle on."

"No. I brought the thermos. It's in the car."

"What? It'll be cold, by now. You hate cold tea."

"It's just ... it's another rule. About visiting here. We're not to eat or drink anything. Ever."

"What has gotten into you?"

"What do you mean?"

"You're not yourself. Look, it's understandable. You're emotional about your—"

"It's not that."

"What is it?" He stepped closer to her and took her arm.

"Have you never noticed it before?" she said, her eyes wide and suddenly child-like. "When we visited here before? When my brother and his family visit?"

"Notice what?"

"We always bring our own food. And our own drinks."

"But that's not unusual. We take our own food to my parents' house, too. Of course we do. With so many mouths to feed ... and mom's always been a terrible cook."

The two rules when visiting Hodgey are 1. Bring Your Own Food, and 2. Never Stay the Night.

. . .

Andrew walked in, thermos in hand. Linda was rummaging throug some brown boxes. "Here's your plastic cup of cold tea."

Linda looked up and smiled. "Thank you."

"I've called the movers and refuse removal company. They'll be her in the morning."

"Already? It seems so soon."

"You're welcome."

Linda was distracted by the contents of a box and didn't reply. Sh held a black and white ribbon in her hand.

"I found a few pieces of furniture worth keeping," he continued. "A oak rocking chair. A cherrywood secretary desk. We can put them i storage for now, till she moves into the new place. Hopefully they' make her feel a bit more at home."

She put the ribbon to the side. "That's great. Thank you."

"You okay?"

Linda looked up, forcing a smile. "Yep."

"Making much progress there? Searching for the family silver?"

"Family silver would come in very handy right now. Peter's found few assisted living facilities. All way out of my budget, of course. He been earning pounds for so long that he can't convert to rand anymore. I asked him to keep looking. Her hospital bills alone will pu me into debt for a year."

"I can't believe she's not on any kind of medical aid."

"Granny Hodge never paid for anything that wasn't absolutel necessary."

"I noticed that none of the toilets had been flushed in a while."

"She sprinkles baby powder in them, instead. Ostensibly to save water."

"She buys non-perishables in bulk. I counted 22 tins of baked beans in the larder."

"She dyes her hair with prune juice."

"What were you looking for, when I came in, just now?"

Linda blew her fringe out of her eyes. "What do you mean?"

"You seemed ... distracted."

"Did I? It's probably just pregnancy-brain."

"You sure?"

She tested a nearby chair for sturdiness, then sat down in it. "I don't know. I do feel a bit weighed down."

"By Hodgey's situation?"

"By the history in here. I mean, this place is brimming with ... well, it's full of dead peoples' things."

Andrew sat down next to her. "Have you found some of your parents' things?"

"Some, yes. But also things from uncle Sid."

"I didn't know you had an uncle."

"He died when we were small. And also things from Hodgey's late husbands."

"Late *husbands*, plural?"

"Yes. She lost two. We never met the first one. Apparently, he wasn't very nice, anyway. I guess everyone loses people."

"I'd say your grandmother lost more loved ones than the average person. And to lose your children ... that must be the worst thing." He swallowed hard. "The worst."

"People used to say that that Hodgey was trailed by grief. It actually became a thing with her. Like, an obsession."

"What do you mean?"

"She began to ... enjoy funerals. Like, she'd scan the local obituary pages and go to strangers' funerals."

"That's bizarre."

"I suppose we're all odd, in our own way."

"Odd?" said Andrew. "Most old people are pretty eccentric, left to their own devices. But I'd say that Hodge sounds bat-shit crazy."

Linda gave Andrew a skew-lipped smile.

He put his hand on her knee. "You ready to go yet? Or are you still stalling?"

"Still stalling," said Linda. "Let me finish sorting through this box, and then we'll go."

When the doorbell rings, it's 7 pm.

"What?" exclaims Linda. "How did it get so late? And who could be at the door?"

"Pizza," said Andrew.

"Hey?"

"I ordered pizza. You're pregnant, and you haven't eaten for hours."

"You're a saint. I love you."

"Go on," said Andrew. "I'll try to dig out the dining room table."

Linda opens the front door. "That's a strange-looking pizza."

"I beg your pardon?" said the old woman with the dramatic eyeliner and purple rinse.

Edna was the eccentric neighbour and Hodgey's best friend. The one who had faded plastic flamingoes in her front garden and black barbed wire wrapped around her orange-brick house. She'd always been grumpy and used to chase her and Peter around with a broom when they were kids. The neighbourhood witch.

"Edna!" said Linda. "How are you?"

"Battling on," she groaned. "Battling on." She slammed her cane down as she walked.

"Come, sit down. I'd offer you a cup of tea, but—"

Linda felt Andrew approach from behind her, so she stepped aside.

"No, no, no, thank you," said the old woman. "Not for me. If I drink tea now, I'll be up all night."

"The caffeine?" asked Andrew.

"The bladder! The old bladder! You know, they don't make them like they used to."

There was an awkward silence.

"Thank you for calling me," said Linda. "About Hodgey."

"I should have called you earlier," Edna said.

"But you called me as soon as the ambulance left. I heard the sirens."

"What I mean is, I should have called you months ago. When she started acting strangely."

"Always been an odd duck, our Hodgey—" said Andrew.

"—but I think something happened. Something changed."

"What do you mean?" asked Linda.

"I don't know. Alzheimer's. Dementia. Although if Larry heard me say that he'd say it's like the sieve saying the colander leaks!"

Edna's husband, Larry, had been dead for years, so Linda took her point.

"She fired Samuel for no discernible reason. You know, the gardener. Been working for us for years, that man. Then, out of the blue, she chases him off the property and throws a rotten apple at him. I saw the whole thing happen."

"It does explain the state of the house," said Linda. "If she fired all her help."

"She was never the best housekeeper," said Edna.

"But this is terrible," Linda said, gesturing around. "Even for her."

Andrew sighed and ruffled his hair. Both women looked at him expectantly.

"What?" asked Linda.

"I didn't want to tell you, but I found some ... bodies. Outside, in the back yard. In black plastic bags."

Linda jolted. "Bodies? What kind of bodies? How could you not tell me?"

"I didn't want to upset you."

"What kind of bodies, for God's sake?"

"I don't know. I didn't want to investigate. Small bodies. Squirrels, or cats. Or especially well-proportioned rats."

Edna nodded, and her nostrils flared. "She was always complaining

bout the feral cats. They'd get into the house — through the broken
windows, no doubt — and chew through packets of food in her larder.
They'd spray. You know, mark their territory. It's difficult to get rid of
that smell, you know. It's especially stubborn, wild cat piss."

A motorbike growled up the driveway; the box on the back was
branded with a cheerful illustration of a pizza. Linda's stomach
growled. "Will you stay for dinner, Edna?"

Oh, we've eaten already, thanks, love. I made Larry's favourite:
haddock and egg pie. I'll be going, then. Just wanted to check in."

We'll go visit Hodge tomorrow morning if you'd like to come along.
Plenty of space in the car."

Oh, no, thank you. No, I won't be doing that."

Linda didn't try to hide her surprise.

Linda, dear, you don't know. Hodgey and I haven't spoken for years."

The next morning, Linda and Andrew had yet to visit Linda's grandmother in the hospital. They had to get the house ready for the refuse
removal team, they agreed. They had to put aside the valuable things
—there weren't many—and they kept finding more boxes to open.
Before they knew it, the men had arrived in their uniforms and heavy-
duty gloves and had shifted most of the household contents into the
skips they had brought along.

Quentin, the team leader, was updating them on their quick progress.
He had a round frame and a Scottish accent. The morning light
caught the red in his beard.

We've got most of the rubbish out, into the skips already. I've ordered
a new one, for the rest. All the good furniture has been wrapped up
and sent to storage. And the clothes and personal effects."

"Thank you," said Linda. "Your team is very efficient."

"It doesn't pay to hang around."

"Yes, I'm sure. Especially in a place like this."

"Och, I've seen worse. I've seen a lot worse."

"Really?"

"I have stories that would scare the bejeezus out of you, lady."

"I'd love to hear them."

Quentin laughed. "Really?"

"She's a writer, you see," said Andrew.

"Ah. Now that explains it. Always looking for stories, eh? Well, min would give you nightmares. Nightmares!"

"I have enough of my own."

"Well, then, let's not exchange them, shall we? You need all the res you can get, by the looks of you."

Linda blinked. "I'll try not to be offended by that remark."

"I just meant your delicate condition, is all. You need to rest up whil you can. I've got three little buggers running around at home, and I ca tell you, sleep is a long forgotten commodity in our house."

Andrew seemed put out by this. Perhaps they'd stick to one "litt bugger".

"How much longer will your team need?"

"We'll try to be out of your hair by sunset."

"Thank you again," said Andrew.

"Oh," said Quentin, scratching his head. "Just a wee coup o'things—"

"Yes?"

"The kitchen things—"

"They can also go. Everything can go."

"It's just that there's a soup kitchen right up the road, you see? At the church."

"Oh, I didn't know."

"They do good work. And I'd hate to just turf out all the food in the larder. There are loads of things that haven't even been opened — flour, sugar, tinned food — not to mention the pots and pans. It would come in really handy at the shelter, I'm sure. They'll collect. You don't have to bother about that. Consider it gone."

"All right, good. That sounds perfect," said Linda. "What was the other thing?"

"Ah. My men set aside a few things—they're in the next room—" Quentin gestured for them to go together, and they followed his lead. "Small things, not things you'd want to be stored with the furniture, I think. But they weren't sure they were junk, either. An old photograph album—my men don't like to throw away photos—and a few bits and bobs."

"What are those strange things?" asked Andrew. "Toy tea set spoons?"

The flush of red on Quentin's skin deepened, and he cleared his throat. "I believe they're ... antique heroin spoons, sir."

Andrew's jaw almost hit the ground. "Heroin?"

"Although she wasn't to know that, was she? They're ancient."

Linda picked up a glass trinket off the table. "Look at this beautiful thing! Handblown glass. So tiny. What is it?"

"I don't know," said Andrew, inspecting it. "A vial, of sorts. Sealed with ... wax?"

"I wonder what this liquid is, inside?"

"God, in this house." Andrew shuddered. "It could be anything."

"Now," said Quentin. "I know you're heading back home tomorrow, but there's an antique fair in town this weekend. Your timing is excellent."

"An antique fair?" said Linda. It wasn't her usual cup of tea, and she was tired.

"If I were you, I'd take this lot along and see what you can get for it. You may be surprised at what some "junk" has been picked up for. That cuckoo clock, for one."

"That horribly kitsch thing?" said Linda. "I'm surprised it's not in the heap outside."

"You'd be surprised, ma'am."

"I suppose that one man's trash is another man's treasure, and all that," said Andrew.

"I think you may be able to get something for it. And they're good, honest people. They won't try to do you in."

Linda was tempted. Having the removal team take care of the dirty work had not come cheap, despite her brother in the UK paying half the bill. Perhaps if she sold the clock she'd be able to offset some of the expenses, even if it was in a small way. They still needed so many things for the baby. At the very least, they'd have somewhere to go for lunch.

The Antique Fair was held on the rugby field of the local high school, and it was a hive of activity. People of all persuasions buzzed around and the smell of cinnamon pancakes and frying doughnuts made Linda's mouth water. The clock was snapped up within minutes.

"Ah, yes, it's a beauty," said the antique dealer. "I'd definitely be interested in that."

Linda looked at the old man in his grey apron and gold-framed specs. "Really?"

"Oh, yes, love. It's a Black Forest original, that clock is. Schwarzwald. All it needs is a little TLC, and I'll give it a good home."

He took a short, blunt pencil from behind his ear and scribbled his offer on a scrap of paper, then passed it to them.

"Wonderful!" said Andrew. Linda and her husband looked at each other, not quite believing their luck.

"Okay. So that's the Chinese silver filigree card case, the brass barley twist candlesticks, the Royal Doulton gravy boat, the silver-footed tray, and the darling clock."

"Yes."

"Would you prefer a cheque or EFT?"

"Don't forget about the glass thing," said Andrew to Linda. "The vial."

"Oh!" said Linda, rifling in her handbag. "Of course. I wrapped it in cotton wool. It looks fragile. "Look at this. Isn't it charming? I don't expect to sell it, but I was interested in its origin."

The antique dealer took it from her and squinted. "Oh, no," he said, "I would never accept this."

"I didn't mean for you to make an offer. I just I thought it was rather quaint—"

"It's not that, love. It is very pretty, indeed. But I know that kind of bottle, and there's only one place it will be welcome."

"Where's that?" asked Andrew.

"The Poison Control Centre."

They finalised their transaction with the dealer and headed to the nearest food truck for a *prego* roll and chips. They found a table in the shade of a tree, one of dozens covered in pretty tablecloths.

"Well," said Andrew. "That went better than expected. I didn't think we'd get anything for that lot.

"Me neither! I guess this lunch is on Hodge."

They tap their bottles of water together.

"It's the bloody least she can do!"

"And a tip for Quentin and his team," said Linda.

"And maybe a cot for the baby," said Andrew, and they looked at each other and held hands.

"I just don't understand why she'd have that poison in the house."

"She probably didn't even know what it was. She liked collecting things, that's all."

"But ... heroin spoons? Poison?"

"It probably just came with the house. You know what those old houses are like. Walls coated in mercury paint and all manner of poisons in the basement. They were pretty free and easy with them in the old days. You'd get arsenic at the local pharmacy, thallium at the grocers'. Any old lady could buy enough poison to fell an elephant for a couple of cents—"

—And without raising any kind of suspicion," said Linda.

Ah, I see," said Andrew, wiping at his mouth with his paper serviette. He pointed at Linda. "You're hatching a new story."

Am I?"

I can always tell. I can see that wicked glimmer in your eye."

Linda laughed. "Don't be ridiculous."

So, you deny it?"

No ... I'm just not sure there's a story, yet."

There's always a story."

On the way home, Andrew turns the car radio down. "Look, I'm not going to nag you."

Good!" said Linda. "What are you not going to nag me about?"

I'm just asking you ... I won't mention it again. I just want to make sure that *you're* sure."

Linda looked out of the window. "I'm sure."

It just seems crazy that we don't visit her while we're here."

I know."

We're not even 10 kilometres away from the hospital. I can turn the car around."

No, let's get home."

Okay. I'm sure you have your reasons. And you've done a lot for her. Sorting out the house. Finding a new place."

Putting myself into a black hole of debt even though I'm about to have a child."

"What I mean, is, you shouldn't feel guilty. About not seeing he
Even though she's your only living relative apart from your brothe
And she's in hosp—"

"—I thought you said you weren't going to nag?"

"I don't mean to push you. I'm just finding it difficult to understand.
mean, we haven't visited her since you fell pregnant."

Linda felt suddenly exhausted. "It's not that I'm *not* going to see he
I'll see her when I'm ready."

A few days later, while Andrew was at work, Linda strolled to th
restaurant up the road. The walk did her good, even though her bac
was still aching when she arrived. Her literary agent was waiting a
the table for her.

"Linda!" she cried, with open arms. "Darling."

"Felicity!"

The agent jumped up, and they hugged. She was looking glamorou
as usual, and Linda self-consciously tugged at her old jacket to hic
the fraying sleeves of the blouse beneath it.

"Look at you!" exclaimed Felicity. "What a beautiful bump! How a
you? How is Brian?"

"Brian?" asked Linda. "Do you mean Andrew?"

"Brian, Andrew, they're all the same at the end of the day, aren
they?"

Linda laughed. Felicity married and divorced more times than sh
changed hairdressers, which was often.

"We're good," said Linda. "We're all good. You?"

"Good! Great! Stressed! Time-starved. Exhausted. You know, th usual. Sometimes I think these bags under my eyes will never go away."

"Which bags?"

"Ah, you're so kind," laughed Felicity and banged the tabletop. "A liar, but a kind liar."

Linda smiled and put her hand on her belly. It wasn't a conscious gesture, it often just floated there of its own accord.

"Wine?" asked Felicity. "I've got a bottle of Riesling here. It's delicious. I've heard that riesling is The New Thing."

"No, thanks," said Linda, patting her bump. "I'm still on the wagon."

"Oh! Of course! Sorry."

"Ah, it's not for much longer. Anyway, more for you!"

They clink glasses and grin at each other.

"I've had an idea," said Linda, playing with the silver fork on the table. "For a new book."

"Well!" said Felicity, throwing back her last sip and topping her glass up. "That *is* good news. I wasn't expecting anything from you while you were..." she gestures in a circular motion at Linda's stomach. "Baking your bun."

"I know. It wasn't planned. The new idea, I mean. I tried to ignore it. It's really not the time to start a new project. But it keeps nagging at me. It wakes me up at night. Or, rather, the baby wakes me up at night, by kicking my ribcage, but then the book idea keeps me awake."

"Tell me more!"

"My grandmother's house. It got me thinking."

"Oh, God, I forgot to ask. How is old Podge?"

"Out of ICU—"

"That's great news."

"—but still in the hospital. They say she'll be ready to go home soon. Her new home, that is."

"Good. Good."

"We found poison. In her house."

Felicity paused, bread roll halfway up to her lips. "Poison? What? Like, rat poison?"

"Maybe."

She put down the roll. "Maybe?"

"Probably. It was in an antique glass bottle. A beautiful thing. And it just started me thinking. You know. What if it wasn't for rats?"

"You want to write about poison? About poisoning people?"

"Not just poison, but about the philosophy of poison."

"'The Philosophy of Poison' — God, I love the sound of that. When can you start?"

"That's why we're friends," said Linda. "You appreciate my disturbed mind. Andrew thinks I'm terrible and dark, you know. He wonders how I come up with such awful things. Especially as I'm about to become the mother of his child. But I just find it fascinating, you know? I mean, it's one thing whipping out a gun and shooting some-one. That out-right kind of violence. Blood and gore. But there is something inherently intriguing to me about the insidiousness of the act of killing someone with food. I mean, the whole point of cooking for someone—to nourish them, to show that you love them—and then you put poison in that food..."

"It's compelling."

Linda stopped playing with the fork and interlaced her fingers. "And then there's the botanical side of it ... poisonous gardens. Shiny black Nightshade berries. Hairy Hemlock."

"A wicked witch's potion garden."

"And the biological side: how the poisoner leaves their indelible mark on their victim. Streaks of toxins in their hair and fingernails. Like, a code. A history you can't erase."

"Look, for what it's worth, I think it's definitely worth exploring. The Philosophy of Poison. Send me a proposal, and I'll take it to Finch."

"I can send more than that. I've already started the research. I couldn't help myself."

"What do you have?"

"Some stories. True crime. I'll dig deeper, of course. But that's where I'm starting. Then..."

"Then?"

"Then, maybe, I'll think of my own. My own story of poison."

~

WIDOW COTTON

BRITAIN, 1873

The widow Mary Ann Cotton was branded the worst mass murderer Britain had ever seen.

West Auckland welfare worker Thomas Riley first became suspicious when Mrs Cotton approached him, asking if he had room in the County

Durham workhouse for her seven-year-old stepson, Charles Edward. The request itself was not unusual—times were tough—and the boy was taking up a bed that could have been let to a lodger.

"The boy," Mary Ann Cotton said, "is in the way."

Riley, the welfare worker, had no space to accommodate Cotton's son. When the child died six days later, Riley approached the police, telling them the boy had been in perfect health the week before. A rushed post-mortem examination was performed before the hearing, but the town doctor found no evidence of foul play. The body was buried in a pauper's grave.

The doctor, however, had kept the contents of the boy's stomach, and when he found time to do a proper chemical analysis, he found distinct traces of arsenic. Widow Cotton was arrested the next morning.

Riley was still suspicious. There had, in fact, been four deaths in the two years where the former nurse had been living. Her late husband, coal-miner Frederick Cotton, had died from 'gastric fever' in September 1871, just two days after the couples' first wedding anniversary. Between March and April the next year, Cotton's ten-year-old son, her 14-month-old infant, and Joseph Nattrass, her former lover, all died under her roof. The three bodies were exhumed, and traces of arsenic were found in all of them.

Newspaper journalists began taking a closer look at the life of Mary Ann Cotton and discovered a horrifying history of an outwardly kind, maternal woman—and devout Methodist—who spread death around her like the plague. At twenty, in Devon, she married a labourer called Mowbray. Together they had five children. Three more children were to be born and to die. Soon Mowbray followed suit.

Her next husband, an engineer, called Wood, died in 1866, only four-teen months after the wedding.

Mary Ann then moved into widower James Robinson's house—as a usekeeper—and soon became pregnant by him, and the pair were arried. His three children, of course, didn't stand a chance. Marching their small graves in quick succession were Robinson's son, ten onths old. Another son, six years old, followed by his sister. Mary nn's biological children didn't fare any better. Nine-year-old Isabella lowbray lost her life, and so did one of her days-old daughters by obinson.

he marriage broke up, leaving Robinson—somewhat surprisingly— ive, after his nifty refusal to take out life insurance. Mary Ann moved n to take care of her sickly mother, and within nine days, she was dead.

lary met her next unlucky lover through his sister. The bigamous arriage was marred only slightly by the sister's death but left the ouple sixty pounds richer.

ltogether, twenty-one people—that we know of—lost their lives in less an twenty years. Mary Ann had given birth to eleven children, but nly one—a girl she gave away—survived. The court could only charge er for the murder of her step-son, Charles, whose life was insured for ght pounds. She was hanged on March 24th, 1873, at the Durham affold. The children sang her song for years afterwards, while skip- ng rope: "Mary Ann Cotton, she's dead and rotten."

~

MARIE LAFARGE

FRANCE, 1840

he 1840 case of Marie Lafarge was one of the most popular arsenic- oisoning stories in 19th century Europe.

larie, a raven-haired beauty, was 24 years old. She was a French aristocrat orphan who was forced into marriage with a duplicitous Charle Defarge, an older man who had painted himself as a successful bus nessman and the owner of a beautiful chateau. Once married, Mar discovered that Charles was, in fact, bankrupt, and the castle was rur down and rat-infested.

There was also the issue of the rather frightening resident mother-i law, and the shock to her refinement of the manner in which her ne husband paid his 'attentions'.

A few months into the marriage, Charles began feeling ill. When h died, his family became suspicious and approached the police, wh arrested Marie.

The beautiful young widow elicited great sympathy at her trial. He lawyer was sure to tell the court of her excellent piano-playing skil and delightful voice, her competence in science and languages, and h Italian poetry. She was also a good actress. She fainted and had to l carried out of court on more than one occasion. Then, a year int proceedings, a renowned toxicologist was called in, and the truth wa discovered. It appeared that the poison for the rats had made their wa into the man's daily bread. By then, Marie's hair was grey, and she ha to be carried in and out of the courtroom on a chaise. She was foun guilty and sentenced to hard labour for life.

There was a gentle knocking on the door, and Linda looked up fro her laptop.

"Don't shoot," joked Andrew. "I brought grilled cheese sandwiches."

"Oh!" said Linda. "I completely lost track of time."

"Sorry to interrupt."

"You're not interrupting."

"It's going well, then, the manuscript?"

"Ah, you know. Still researching. I'm trying to find my way."

Andrew nodded and was about to say something when Linda snapped her laptop shut. "I need to tell you something."

Andrew was still standing at the door with the tray. "I don't like the sound of that."

"I have to tell you, so that you understand. The reason we always took our own food to Hodgey's house. The reason we never stayed the night."

"Because her cooking was awful. Her beds were lumpy. Her house was haunted. And it smelled funny."

Andrew's smiling, but Linda's face is grey. "Apart from that."

"You've got my attention."

"When we used to stay there. Peter and I, as kids. The house *was* kind of haunted ... in a way."

"I knew it!"

"Granny Hodge. She was the one."

"She was the one who what?"

"The one who ... made bad things happen."

"Sweet, mad old Hodgey? What do you mean?"

"She used to ... put things in our food."

"—in your—? Like what?"

"We never knew. We never spoke about it. We just knew that if we stayed there, we would pass out after lunch and not wake up for hours and hours. She was always begging us to stay the night."

"You're saying Hodge would ... drug you?

"I don't know. We weren't even sure if it was true. I mean, how could it be true? Wonderful, warm Granny Hodgepodge. Sometimes it would be our stomachs. Maybe she used laxatives or something. We always seemed to come down with something when we were there. And then we'd stay over, just like she wanted us to."

"You weren't sure then. What about now?"

"I wouldn't be able to prove it if that's what you mean."

"But you agreed with Peter to not eat her food."

"Yes. When we were sixteen. When we lost Mom and Dad."

"And since then, no passing out? No sickness?"

"Yes."

"I'd say that's your proof, right there."

"But it doesn't make any *sense*. It's a difficult thing to wrap your head around. What reason could she have had? God, we loved her! How can you love such a wicked person? Once, when her vision was starting to fail, she made us some French toast. There was this white powder on it."

"It wasn't icing sugar. Jesus Christ."

"We didn't wait to find out. Chucked it out of the window when she wasn't looking. That's when we promised each other ..."

"And those half-melted heroin spoons?" said Andrew. "And the vial of poison? It wasn't an accident that we found those in her house. That's probably the least of it. That house is probably layered with different kinds of poisons. God, those bags of dead animals..."

He slammed the tray onto her desk in disgust, making Linda jump.

"The vial is what started me thinking," said Linda.

"About the book?"

"About the abuse. Because that's what it was, wasn't it?"

Andrew didn't hesitate to answer. "Yes."

"So ... insidious ... that we never even knew we were being abused. That we never knew enough to confront it. And it didn't stop at us, of course. I mean, Peter and I."

"What do you mean?"

"Her husbands died, didn't they? Both of them. Under her roof."

"Now, that may be jumping to conclusions."

"There are no conclusions. That is what makes this infuriating. But two husbands. Who ate her cooking every day of their lives. And what about Uncle Sid? He died there, too. He was so young!"

The blood drained from Andrew's face and left him looking as white as wax. He slumped down into a chair and put his hand to his temple. "Your ... parents," he said. "It was a car accident."

"Yes," said Linda, her jaw tightening. "A car accident. On their way home from Hodge's house."

Andrew left the cold sandwiches in Linda's office and went to pour himself a stiff drink and make a cup of tea. Linda opened her laptop again, created a new document, and started typing.

No one thought it suspicious when Linda Harrison, at seven months pregnant, parked outside her ill grandmother's house, which had been boarded up and plastered with 'FOR SALE' signs. The neighbour, Edna Ruth, was washing the supper dishes from the night before and lifted her yellow hand in a soapy wave, but Linda did not see her.

The key was in the same place as always, and Linda let herself in through the front door. She made her way through to the kitchen, where she found everything she needed, and the oven, still in working order. The eggs, milk and butter, she had brought herself. For the other ingredients, she helped herself from her grandmother's pantry and then threw all the other food away.

Once the cookies were baked and cooled, Linda slid them carefully into the gift box she had brought and tied it with the black and white ribbon she had found on her last visit. She took the cookies with her and left the house smelling of freshly baked cookies, never to return.

Linda walked down the hospital hallway, gift box in hand, black and white ribbon swaying. She greeted a nurse and asked for her grandmother's room.

"Ah, dear Mrs Hodge!" The nurse had lipstick on her teeth. "We were wondering when she'd get a visitor, poor dear. She's *desperate* for company."

Linda waited patiently for the room number, but the nurse sniffed the air and looked at the box. "And you've brought her some treats! What a darling you are. She'll love those. She'll just love those."

"Which way is it, to her room?"

"You're Linda, aren't you? She knew you'd come, you know. She kept telling us. Down that corridor there, through the double door. She's in 24A, that's the second on your right."

Linda thanked the nurse and walked through the double doors.

Linda Harris stood outside her grandmother's door, her fist suspended in the air, as if she was about to knock, but something held her back. In her other hand, the gift box became damp with perspiration. Her thoughts were difficult to grasp. Pictures and sensations flashed in on er mind: *Her mother's easy laugh, her father's cigarette smoke. Peter on is bashed-up blue bike.*

,inda remembered Granny Hodge gently combing and braiding her air for her parents' funeral, tying it carefully with a black and white bbon.

: was the baby in her belly that brought Linda Harrison back to life. 'he kick in her ribs woke her up, still standing there with her white nuckles at the hospital room door. She lowered her hand and turned ound to leave. With his kicking, the baby was asserting himself; sserting the cycle of life. Linda dropped the unopened box of cookies to the hospital waste chute. She heard it tumble deep into the building nd then drove home, stopping only to buy a baby crib on the way.

∼

8

COMET

When I saw my schnauzer that afternoon, I almost spontaneously combusted. It was a sudden bright fury that overtook my body and made my brain sizzle in my skull.

"What. Have. You. Done?" I demanded, through gritted teeth.

Comet cocked his head and looked at me, wondering what the fuss was about. Maybe he thought he looked stylish with his new haircut; I certainly did not.

Hairdryers blasted hot air in the pet salon; the scent of shampoo got right up my nose.

"Uh," said the dog groomer, in her ridiculously frilly apron. It was a garish pink, and had an amateur illustration of a happy dog on it, with hearts for eyes. She looked at me nervously, and her eyes darted from me to my dog, and back to me again. It was as if she was deciding which wire to cut to disarm a ticking bomb. I found everything about her ridiculous. It seemed that she had transferred some of her crackpot aesthetics to Comet, for which I would never forgive her. Not until his hair grew back, anyway.

"What exactly were you going for?" I asked. Usually, the schnauzer was so handsome; I received compliments about him wherever I went. Now he'd be ashamed if he knew how he looked. What would I tell people?

"Were you trying to shave the atlas on his coat? Craters on the moon? Or is it some kind of abstract art?"

The groomer looked at me, lips slightly ajar, but silent. *Tick tock,* went the explosive between us.

My jaw began to ache with the anger that was wiring it shut. These bloody people with their bloody clippers and no bloody idea what they were doing. Comet whined and cocked his head the other way. Did the ridiculous person not have any vocal cords? Or was she just being insolent?

"Well?" I demanded. "Is it art?"

"No?" replied the pink apron, blinking at me.

Some of the other groomers stopped what they were doing to watch the crazy rich woman who seemed as if she was about to detonate.

"Exactly!" I hissed. "All I wanted was a neat trim, and you've made him look like he's suffering from the bloody plague!"

Pink apron was about to say something but changed her mind.

My suspicion kindled. "You young people. You're doing that Bird Box challenge, aren't you?"

She frowned. "Bird Box?"

"When you blindfold yourself and then do something stupid. Tell me the truth," I said, gesturing at Comet. "Did you do this blindfolded?"

The groomer shook her head, her stubborn silence adding fuel to my fury. She glanced at the dog as if he would back her up in some way, but I could tell he was beginning to get the idea. He was starting to understand that, despite his excellent breeding, he currently looked like a mangey pavement special. I wondered if I should get him a cone for his neck so that he wouldn't have to witness this new, burning humiliation. We'd cancel our plans. We'd stay at home until he felt less ashamed of his awful appearance. Poor boy.

"I don't think I should pay for this," I said, shaking my head while I wrenched my wallet from my handbag and violently zipped it open. "In fact, I think YOU should be paying ME."

The frills on the apron ruffled as the warm air from the hairdryers reached us. It was the only part of her that moved; the rest of the ridiculous woman may as well have been made of wax.

"Damages," I said. "You should be paying me damages."

I passed the groomer my credit card, and she took it from me cautiously, as if it were a test. As if it were a pin of a grenade. I held onto it for a moment longer and stared at her, to reiterate my point. When I finally let go, she didn't take her eyes off me as she tapped the card on the machine. It spat out a paper slip. I scooped Comet up and held him under my arm, kissing the uneven fur on top of his head. As I headed for the exit, I heard the woman call after me.

"Thank you for visiting Shampooch," she said. "Have a nice day!"

I stopped in my tracks, ready to cut her down with a contemptuous comment, but then I remembered myself. I swept out of the door, into the sunbaked parking lot, and despite the BMW's powerful air conditioning, I simmered all the way home.

A week later, Comet's appearance had not improved. In fact, he looked worse than ever. I found his hair all around the house, and when I washed him, his hair clogged up the drain.

"I'm going to sue that bloody dog parlour," I seethed.

Grant cracked a beer open and laughed. "Sue them? For what?"

"For this!" I said, showing my husband the brush I used to groom Comet. It was full of dull dog hair. "He's embarrassed about how he looks! It's distressing. His hair is literally falling out."

Grant threw back his head and laughed, which made me even angrier.

I slammed the brush down on the table. "Don't act as if you don't care about him!"

Grant was the one who had wanted to adopt him—and his sister, Nova —in the first place, the one who played fetch with them, the one who took the pair of sibling schnauzers for proper walks, and to chase tennis balls at the park. Grant was the one who bought them matching teddy bears to carry around the house in their jaws, and to cuddle in bed. In some ways, they were closer than we were. I envied their uncomplicated relationship.

"Look," he said, sprawling on the couch in that infuriatingly relaxed way of his. All smiles and long, muscular limbs. "I don't think he cares about his coat."

"How can you say that?" I demanded. "Comet is an extremely intelligent animal."

Grant put up his hands in surrender. "I know," he said. "I know. But I'm just saying that maybe you're projecting *your* stress onto him. That's all. He might even like his new look. I saw him eyeing himself in your mirror the other day."

"What rubbish," I said. I tried to stay cross, but a laugh bubbled up in my throat.

"He was!" said Grant. "He was smiling and had a sparkle in his eye, I swear. I was almost expecting him to wink at his reflection."

It was so absurd; I had to laugh. Grant was such a useless husband in so many ways, but the number of times he had talked me down from a iff made up for it. While I was a ball of fury, he was a cool brook. Without his jokes, I'm sure I would be so brittle I would have broken a half by then, or shattered into tiny shards. I looked at Comet and roked his ears. He had Nova's teddy in his mouth.

Who's a good boy?" I said, and he barked and thumped his tail.

rant was a wonderful husband and a great provider, but sometimes e wasn't that good at being a responsible adult. This was a man who ad planted a tree upside down once. He thought the roots were the ranches. Another time, he told me the vacuum cleaner had stopped orking. I showed him how to empty the bag, and he was amazed. Despite being quite smart and quick-witted, I had the suspicion he lought that vacuum cleaners make dust just magically disappear.

One night he went out to buy toothpaste because we had just run out. He came home with ice cream, M&Ms, candy-striped facecloths that ad been on sale, a jigsaw puzzle—but no toothpaste.

couple of years ago we were at the Westcliff Hotel for a high tea ith friends. Grant was eyeing the carrot cake.

What do they put in carrot cake to make it taste like carrots?" he sked, loud enough for the whole table to hear. When they started ughing, he said, "Is it carrot zest?"

uffice to say; they have never let him live that one down.

When we first moved in together, we had a small housewarming. I rapped potatoes in tinfoil for the *braai*. Grant ran out of space on the arbecue coals, so he decided to cook them in the microwave, instead. He sprinted up the stairs asking if it was normal to have "lightning olts" in the microwave. When I came down to check, I saw he hadn't emoved the foil. We had to buy a new microwave. It's not the only ppliance he's killed.

One morning I was woken by this terrible acrid smell: burning plastic. Before I could jump out of bed to investigate, Grant rushed in. "I've done something really stupid," he said.

The fact he admitted this was alarming, to say the least.

"I promise I'll fix it."

"It" was my limited edition designer copper kettle, the one I had paid thousands for, just because it was charming. It sat on our kitchen counter, looking grand, too beautiful to use. To boil water, we used the stove-top kettle on our gas plates. Grant had been half-asleep when he put the kettle on that morning—at least, that's what he told me. He had put my beautiful copper kettle on the gas flames, not realising it had mostly plastic base.

I like to tell the story at parties, but not to make him feel bad. I forgave him the moment he rushed in with that panicky expression on his face, leaving smoke in his wake. I would forgive him anything, really. After all, I was grieving, and he had been trying to make me a cup of tea.

Two weeks after the incident at Shampooch, Comet looked just awful. He carried Nova's teddy bear wherever he went.

"I just don't know what to think," I told Grant. "I mean, what did they do to him? Did they mix up their bottles of depilatory cream and shampoo? Do you even get depilatory cream for pets?"

Grant narrowed his eyes and rubbed his lips as he thought it over. "Probably," he decided. "A unibrow would not look good on a chihuahua."

I stared at Comet, his coat an absolute disaster of bald patches and unattractive fuzz. Islands of dull fur stood out from his exposed pink skin.

"We should just shave him," said Grant.

"*Shave* him?" I said. "Are you crazy?"

"It would look better that ... *that*," he said. "It's falling out anyway. We can just neaten him up. Front, back and sides."

"There is no way I'm taking him back to that godforsaken pet salon," I said. "They're lucky I haven't had them shut down."

"We can shave him," said Grant. "We'll just use my electric thingie."

I thought of the vacuum cleaner, the lightning bolts in the microwave, and my beautiful copper kettle, scorched and—reluctantly—consigned to the bin. "Not a chance," I said, shaking my head.

Shampooch was not an option, but there was no way I was going to let Grant anywhere near the poor schnauzer with his shaver. I wasn't going to let Comet get any more traumatised than he already was. He looked at me and whined.

"We need a dog whisperer," I said, and Grant threw his head back and roared with laughter.

"A dog whisperer?" He was laughing so hard his eyes began to stream.

I wasn't deterred. "A canine psychologist," I said. "I'll Google for recommendations."

"Are you being serious?" Grant asked, wiping his tears away. "You know that dogs can't actually talk, right?"

"Yes," I said, typing "dog whisperer" into my phone.

Two days later, we were sitting in the Dog Psychologist's office. When the receptionist called us, we entered a comfortable looking lounge littered with old tennis balls and chewy rubber bones that squeaked as you tripped over them, as Grant did when he crossed the threshold.

Doctor Lebrassi was an eccentric looking man. He had Einstein hair and round black-rimmed glasses. I let Comet out of his carrier, and he seemed instantly at home, chasing down a yellow ball. The psychologist shook our hands with both of his, then clapped to start the session.

He called Comet over and scrubbed his chin with gentle fingers. "What a beautiful dog you are," he said, looking into his sweet eyes. "What a lovely boy."

"He used to be beautiful," I said. "Before that pet salon got hold of him."

The doctor didn't take his eyes off Comet. He kept stroking him as he examined his patchy coat.

"But that was weeks ago," said Grant. "And he just keeps losing hair."

The doctor took a few more moments to examine Comet, looking at his gums, teeth, and massaging his coat, looking for any abnormalities, then he gave him a treat from his jacket pocket and told him to play.

"There is good news," Lebrassi said, adjusting his glasses. He spoke in an accent that seemed slightly Italian, but I wasn't sure.

"What's the bad news?" Grant wanted to know.

"He has experienced a trauma," said the dog psychologist.

I ground my teeth. Those bloody dog groomers."It was at the doggie parlour," I said. I wanted to kill them.

Doctor Lebrassi shook his head. "No. It is a deep wound — not a bad day at a doggie parlour. Something else has happened to him, something truly traumatic. His body is manifesting the stress, hence the hair fall."

"Oh," I said, and Grant looked at me. We knew exactly what it was. A lump rose in my throat, so Grant had to continue.

"Comet's sister died a few months ago. They were best friends. They were always together."

At least it was a peaceful death, we told ourselves. No accident, no shock, just a slow descent as her health deteriorated, and we had her put to sleep. We had laid down her favourite blanket on the cold steel table at the vet and placed her shuddering body there. We tucked her favourite teddy under her front leg—the way she liked it—and sobbed in each others' arms as the drugs took effect and her breathing slowed and then stopped. The loss had been devastating for all of us. Comet had searched every nook of the house for days and howled into the night for his best friend, which had just made us cry more.

"I'm sorry for your loss." Lebrassi gave us a tender smile. "Comet will recover in time, and so will you." He slapped his knees. "That's the good news." He leaned down to pick up a rope from the carpet and threw it for Comet to fetch. The schnauzer did so and brought it back, wagging his tail like a puppy.

I blinked back the tears.

"So what do we do?" asked Grant.

"I prescribe plenty of play," said the doctor, "plenty of cuddling, and plenty of treats." He brought out another dog biscuit from his pocket and gave it to Comet, ruffling the fur he had left sprouting unevenly on his head.

"And his hair will grow back?" I asked, finally able to talk past the tears.

"Definitely," said Lebrassi, looking pleased.

"Do you recommend any kind of medicated shampoo or anything like that?" I asked. "You know, to speed it up?"

The psychologist walked to his desk and scribbled on a piece of paper.

"This oil may help," he smiled. "But you're going to have to go back to that doggie parlour to get it."

In the car on the way home, I told Grant there was no way that I was going back to Shampooch for the prescribed oil. Even thinking about walking in there made my cheeks burn.

"You should go," he said. "To apologise."

"I know," I said, "but I'm not going to."

He dropped Comet and I off at home and set off for the pet salon.

"Grant!" I called, as he started up the car again. He wound down his window. "Ask them how to use it."

"Yes, ma'am," he said, tipping an imaginary hat.

"And listen to what they say," I said, but he had already closed the window and was accelerating down the driveway.

When he arrived back you'd swear he was carrying an Ironman trophy, so broad was the grin on his face.

"I got it!" he said—rather unnecessarily, I thought—as he was brandishing the box so proudly. I bit back a snide comment and instead smiled and thanked him. We covered Comet head to tail in the stuff, taking care to rub the oil in gently but thoroughly. It was a small bottle, and we used the whole thing. I didn't want to miss a spot. It wasn't easy, though, because the oil smelled absolutely disgusting.

"Ugh," I said, covering my mouth and nose with the crook of my arm, and Grant had an appalled look on his face. We took turns to take breaks outside for fresh air. We finished the job, trying not to heave, and it was a relief to peel off our gloves and bin them and send Comet outside, to the back lawn, for a run.

"I've never smelled anything so revolting in my life," I said, holding my chest. "What do they put in that stuff?"

"Dead skunks," joked Grant. "Public toilet deodorisers. And essence of upchuck."

"Don't," I said, pretending to retch. "I'll be sick."

"Jokes aside," said Grant. "It's the worst thing I've ever smelt."

"Ugh," I said again, in agreement. "When can we wash it out?"

Grant looked at his watch. "Not yet."

"What are we going to do?" I asked, and Grant frowned at me.

"We can't leave him out there, and we can't bring him inside."

After a stiff drink, we decided to cover all the furniture in old towels and blankets. We let Comet in, and went out to dinner. When we came back, the house reeked to high heaven. Just by opening the front door we were hit by a wall of stench so bad we both gasped and covered our noses.

"I'm going to be sick," I said, grasping my stomach. I instantly regretted the mussels in garlic cream sauce I'd eaten at the restaurant. Poor Comet lay on the covered couch, looking dismayed at the putrid odour he was emitting.

"Can we wash it off now?" I asked. Grant said he'd check, and ran to the kitchen, where the product's packaging was. When he returned, he nodded. "Yep," he said. "Yep. We can wash it off."

I ran a deep bath in the guest ensuite and loaded the schnauzer with dog shampoo while Grant collected all the towels and put them in the washing machine. We had to wash Comet four times before he smelled—almost—normal again.

"This oil better bloody work," I said as I dried him off. I desperately wanted Comet's hair to grow back, but I wasn't sure I could go through with this rigmarole again. I cleaned up, fed him, and tucked him up into his basket with Nova's teddy.

"I know you miss Nova," I said to him, stroking his head. "We all do. She was a wonderful dog. But it won't always hurt this much. We'll all feel better soon and your hair will grow back."

Comet looked at me in that way only dogs can, and I felt my heart swell with affection for him. "Good night," I whispered, kissing his head. "Don't let the bedbugs bite."

They'd have to be extremely unfortunate bedbugs, I thought, to go anywhere near him.

When I found Grant sitting outside on the patio—the house still reeked, despite the towels churning in the washing machine—I knew by the way he looked at me and bit his lip that he was about to confess something.

"What is it?" I asked. Before waiting for an answer, I walked to the kitchen and fished the packaging of the medicated oil out of the bin. I turned it around and looked at the instructions.

"Graaaant!" I yelled.

There was only one line, and it was easy to understand.

Add 2 - 3 drops of oil to dog's food, once a day.

9

WITCHES GET STITCHES

This short story takes place before 'Blood Magic', which is a completed six-book urban fantasy series.

The main character is Jacquelyn Denna Knight, who grows up to be a wizard detective who solves paranormal cases (and slays vampires in her spare time).

~

I was standing on our front lawn, having just returned from the neighbour's birthday party next door. I could still taste the Oros juice and the Cheese Curls, the popcorn and cake. I was wearing yellow shorts and a My Little Pony T-shirt. I hesitated as if I somehow knew what awaited me—a dreamlike *deja vu*. I didn't want to step forward, but something forced me. Soon I saw my strawberry glitter jelly sandals swinging out before me as I walked towards the front door.

Something was different. Something felt wrong. I knew it before I entered the house. That was the first time I smelled that scent. The smell that fills me with dread and dangerous thoughts.

Crimson copper.

I called for my parents and looked in the kitchen for them, in the garden, in the study, but they didn't answer. Their bedroom door was closed. I knocked on it.

"Mom?" I said. "Dad?"

Still no answer.

I stood there for a while, not sure what to do. Perhaps they were sleeping? I tried the handle, but the door was locked.

"Mom?"

Starting to get worried, I dropped my party pack on the carpet and wrapped my fingers around the doorknob. The metallic blood smell was much stronger now, and I knew for sure something was wrong. I had never melted a lock before. Mom and Dad had told me that I was only to do it in an emergency. I wasn't sure if it was an emergency, but it felt like one.

"Ignem exquiris," I said. The heat from my spell softened the metal of the lock just enough for me to force the door open, and what I saw made my mouth stretch into a scream.

"No!" I shouted, sitting up in my bed, my heart sprinting. Half asleep, I prepared to defend myself from the imminent threat that had haunted me every day since my parents were killed. I snatched my mother's antique silver wand from my bedside table. My dorm was dark and cold, and my breath came out as white vapour. It gradually dawned on me that it had been a dream; a memory that would never leave me in peace. I'd often have nightmares when I was nervous about something, so it all made sense.

I had been practising archery every day for a year. That day was the National Magical School Championship. It was a big day for me, and the whole school would be watching. I would be representing The Copperfield Institute, the most accomplished magical school on the continent. I breathed deeply to slow my mad heart, trying to calm down. I ran my fingers through my hair, but ... it was gone

"What the *faex?*" I looked down at my pillow and saw a nest of my hair. There was barely any left on my head.

I heard giggling in the hostel passage. I shot out of bed; fear morphing quickly to anger. The adrenaline jetting through my body allowed me to practically fly through the air, into the dormitory opposite mine, where I found three giggling witches. At least they had the grace to look alarmed when they saw me.

Isadora Crowe—spiteful, smug Izzy—looked at the sharp silver scissors in her hand and muttered something under her breath. There was the faint sound of a finger-click, and the scissors vanished.

"You," I sneered. "You *filius canis!*"

Filius canis means 'son of a bitch'. I probably could have thought of a more appropriate curse word for the witch, but my fury seemed to be sending little electric impulses into my brain.

"You," Izzy said, her voice sharp with contempt. "*Wizard.*"

The silver wand was growing warm, and I felt the power rising in my chest.

My name is Jacquelyn Denna Knight, and I turn my pain into magic.

"*Fiat Fulgur!*" I yelled, and a bolt of white lightning surged within me, bypassing my heart and shooting out of my hand, hurtling through the wand and into the wall, just missing the shrieking witch. It exploded a hole in the panel and sent a billowing cloud of golden, glittering smoke into the air. The witches looked horrified.

"You could have killed her!" shouted Selena.

"It would have been good riddance," I said. Of course, I didn't mean it. I just wanted to scare them. I needed them to stop with their stupid pranks and witches' tricks. I'd had enough, and I wanted them to know it. I wasn't some meek orphan who'd roll over and play dead. I had fought for survival, and I would fight them, too.

"You're so *weird*," said Lilith, but I ignored her. I'd rather be a weird wizard than a bland little yay-saying witch.

Besides, I'd heard it all before:

You're weird.

Girls aren't supposed to be wizards.

Street urchin!

Nobody wants you.

You don't belong here.

"You put superglue in my tooth-whitening paste last week," I said to Crowe.

She shook her head. "I didn't. I didn't!"

My instinct told me it was her, and it was not often wrong. But I needed proof. I stared at her, my stomach roiling with fury. Without meaning to, angry magic flowed out of my fingers, waiting for my command. I had none. My hands sparked blue as I tried to calm down. It felt as if my magic was trying to jump out of my skin.

Ventum exquiris, I heard myself think, without meaning to. Soon a ind whipped up inside the room, sending objects flying around us in whirlwind of juvenile magic.

What are you doing?" demanded Crowe, cowering to protect herself om being hit by the flying objects. "Stop it. Stop it!"

ut my anger would not abate. The hurricane got stronger. Light owed from my palms and joined the sweeping wind, till the gust was ot through with blue. Soon the cupboard doors flew open, and the est of drawers smashed into the wall opposite. The contents went ying around the room, including a packet of condoms, a box of ciga- ttes, and a half-empty tube of superglue.

mpedio!" I shouted, and the objects froze in the air around us. They utched their chests in a melodramatic way as I plucked the super- ue from between us and showed it to Crowe. Annoyed, she set her w and glared at me.

Fine," she said, through gritted teeth. "It was me."

And?"

And I won't do it again." Her eyes flickered with hostility.

felt I had made my point. I dropped the tube of glue, and as it fell, e other suspended objects fell, too, raining down on the shaken itches.

turned to stride back to my dorm but came face-to-face with Ms. Took, the strictest house mistress at the Copperfield Institute. Just my ck.

Ms. Knight," she said, arms folded. "That's an interesting haircut."

ly hands flew up to my short hair. "Er," I said. We weren't allowed to se magic around the hostel, but it would mostly be overlooked if it was inoffensive. But using magic against a fellow student was a whole different quiver of arrows.

"You'll have detention this afternoon," she announced, looking down her crooked nose at me.

"No!" I shouted. "It's the national championship today! And I didn't even do anything wrong. I was just sticking up for myself—"

"Swearing," she said.

"It was in Latin!"

"Nonetheless: Swearing; spell-slinging; scrimmaging. You're lucky I'm not grounding you for the rest of the term."

"If I can compete in the championship today," I pleaded, "you can ground me for the rest of the year."

Ms. Hook looked at me with her cold eyes, as if trying to decide. I rearranged my face into the most contrite expression I could manage.

"No," she said. She turned on her heel and marched off. I had never been very good at acting.

I hated Izzy Crowe and her rotten teenage coven; despised them so much I felt I had a flame inside my stomach. I knew if I lost my temper again, there would be severe consequences. The school bell rang, signalling our first class would start in two minutes, but I couldn't face sitting at a desk with all that anger simmering inside me. Instead, I went to the bathroom and whipped out my wand. Channelling my feelings into the silver spellstick, I gathered my thoughts and said under my breath, "*Fervens.*"

I had learnt the spell from my Latin lessons with old Bent Neck. Do you know how they say Latin is a dead language? Professor Bender was a living example of how dead things can be dragged into the twenty-first century. We would have called him a coffin-dodger, but it appeared that he had hardly dodged said coffin; he had one foot squarely in there, and the other hovering indecisively above it, like a cat at an open door.

I felt my powers streaming through my body, and it felt good. I used my anger at Izzy, my heartbreak over my parents, and my sadness at never fitting in. I had lost the place I had ever truly belonged—my parents were both wizards, and I had a happy childhood—but that was all taken away from me. The spell got stronger, and the flame at the tip of the wand turned from a gentle fire into a hissing blue blade of a blowtorch. I used the fever torch to burn letters into the back of the door, the scented smoke swirling up to the ceiling.

WITCHES GET STITCHES

When I had finished, I blew out the flame and felt simultaneously guilty and relieved. I may get extra detention, but at least I wouldn't have to spend the day pushing down the anger and sadness I felt.

Late for class, I quickly pocketed my wand and rushed along the corridor. The classes were already underway, and all the classroom doors were closed. I turned the corner and ran through the quad, but stopped when I saw the copper statue of Minerva. I had seen the statue almost every day since my arrival at The Copperfield Institute, so I don't know what happened that day to stop me. I walked up to it, thinking about the Myth of Minerva's Owl.

We never could agree on what finding that ephemeral hooting owl hidden in the folds of the robes of the copper statue would get you, but we knew it would be good luck in some form or another. No one I knew had ever actually seen the owl, so when I noticed its feathered head just peaking out from the cloak, I had to look twice. Everything was so quiet around us as I laid my palm on the bird's cool, shaded head. Would this give me the much-desired luck I needed? I always thought that superstitions existed for a reason; even if it was just to light up your day with hope. Like having the giant Jacaranda raining purple blossoms on you in exam time, promising good results, and the Kissing Arch twin trees in the third quad, where nailing your shoes to the bark ensured you and your beau would be lifelong lovers. Or putting a white crayon on your windowsill and a silver coin under your pillow to bring on a snow day. We did it knowing full well that snowfall in Johannesburg is as rare as good dental hygiene in an orc, but we did it anyway with the vague wish that one day it would come true.

I have learned since that Untouched—non-magical—psychologists call the phenomena "magical thinking"; perhaps they don't know how close they are to seeing what lies beyond the shimmering veil of the Masquerade.

People in Johannesburg are forever saying how cosmopolitan the city is, how we're so lucky to have such a melting pot of skin colours, languages, and cultures. But what most humans who aren't touched by magic don't know is that there are thousands of magical creatures living amongst them. We call it the Masquerade, and the illusion is to be protected at all costs. Basically, all that means is that the muggles—I mean, the Untouched—don't have a cooking clue, and we need to keep it that way. If we do a good job, the Untouched will continue believing that they are the only humanoids on the planet. Ha! Can you imagine that? Can you imagine a world without magic? It must be like living in black and white, with blinkers on. Colour-blind and narrow-sighted, and depressing as hell. Regular humans think that it's "science" that keeps their crops green and their planes from falling out of the air. What they don't know is that there is a vast source of magic out there, of energy, that can be tapped into for good and evil. They don't know that if the Void were to disappear overnight, there would be untold repercussions in the Untouched world. It's not that science isn't magic

—it is—it's more that if there were no magic, there would be no science. And without advanced tech, well, we'd be without a lot of different branches of magic. Dwarves, like Ferra, are particularly good at harnessing science to augment their magic. I use something less technical. I was born with the ability to transform my emotion into sorcery. I find that pain is extraordinarily powerful. It's the major tenet on which Blood Magic is based: power from pain, preferably from someone else. But I've never been into the Dark Arts. I use my own suffering instead.

I have also learned that sometimes good luck comes disguised as bad. When I was homeless after the attack, I fell in with the Ferals. The Ferals were the street kids in the Johannesburg inner-city, and I owed my life to them. There I was, a traumatised little white girl who had only ever known middle-class suburbia—and a bit of simple magic, like clapping my bedroom light on and off—with a little to zero chance of surviving on the streets. But the Ferals took me in, toughened me up, and taught me what I needed to know to avoid becoming a victim. From the Ferals, I learnt parkour, and quick and dirty magic, perfect for picking pockets and sneaking stolen food, essential for our survival. From the Copperfield Institute, I was learning the more academic side of sorcery: elementary magic, and traditional Latin incantations. The combination has made for an interesting arsenal of spells.

Standing in front of Minerva, with my hand on the owl's head, I was so caught up in the garbage-scented memories that I didn't hear anyone approach. When she tapped me on my shoulder, I must have shot a foot in the air.

"Shouldn't you be in class, young lady?" said the dwarf.

"Ferra!"

She winked at me; her eyes bright nutmegs flecked with gold. She was in her Head Matron uniform: denim dungarees, an oversized white apron, and a Viking helmet. Her Scot-red hair was plaited into pigtails.

When we had first met at the Institute, Ferra took me under her wing, and I'd been there ever since. She was tender-hearted to all the orphans, but we had a special connection. She'd sneak me extra spice cookies and give me magical science books to read.

"Eat up, Jinx," she would say, using my favourite nickname. "You're too skinny." And, "When in doubt, have the cookie. You never know when it will be your last."

"Happy birthday," said Ferra, and gave me one of her rib-crushing hugs.

"It's not my birthday."

"It is, now," said Ferra. "I'm officially assigning this day as your birthday, and from now on we'll celebrate it every year!"

I blinked away the salt water that had suddenly sprung to my eyes—stupid tears.

I only noticed then that Ferra was holding a gift in her hand. The wrapping paper had little animated dragons on it, breathing out little sparks and plumes of smoke. They were cute to watch, and I hesitated to tear the paper.

"Go on," urged Ferra, looking at her ticking steampunk-themed watch. "We don't have all day!"

The gift was especially poignant because I knew that Ferra saved every cent she could. She had big plans for her future; dreams of opening a bold, beautiful magical pub and restaurant and having a big family. She had been saving her Copperfield salary for years and never

ent any money on herself. I sniffed and tore open the paper. What I
w took my breath away.

No," I said, shaking my head. "I can't accept this. No way!"

lack and sleek, it was the most beautiful crossbow I had ever seen in
y life. As if feeling the magic in my hands, it began vibrating in a low
equency, as if it were purring. It was too much.

t must have cost a fortune," I said. "I can't—"

've been working on it for months," said Ferra, her face shining.

ou made this?" I asked. I shouldn't have been surprised because
erra had one of the best engineering minds in the Realm, and was
rever building things in her makeshift workshop.

Thank you," I said, the crossbow humming in my hands.

You're very welcome, skunk," she said. I think she would have ruffled
y new short hair if she'd been tall enough.

t's a shame I won't be using it in today's championship," I said. "I've
ot detention."

erra's red wiry eyebrows knitted together as she frowned. "Well," she
id, "we'll just see about that." She slung her tea towel over her
oulder and marched off in the direction of Directress Copperfield's
fice.

he bell rang for the next lesson, so I quickly slipped into the stream
f students and attended the next few classes: Theory of Magic;
ledge Chemistry; Potions; Occult History.

Vhen the directress appeared in our classroom, we knew the lesson
ould be an important one. Suffice to say we'd sit up straight if she
alked in to give a lesson. She was an intimidating figure; flawless
ahogany skin and ivory-coloured braids and wand. She was eighty in

the shade, had a world-renowned titanium wand—which ju
happened to match her spine. You could say anything you liked abou
the Institute, but for as long as Directress Copperfield was there, yo
knew it was beyond reproach.

"You need to always consider the keel," she said, as she looked me i
the eye. I didn't know what a "keel" was so I just stared right back, ea
on stalks.

"Consider the keel," she said again. She used her wand as a piece
chalk and drew a simple sailboat in the air before us. She tapped at th
bottom of the boat, and it turned upside down.

"The upside-down, the flip-side, the *is* that *isn't*."

We gawked back at her with our mouths open. We still didn't kno
what she was talking about. The directress waved away the air sketc
and shook her head.

"In fact," said the directress, walking across the room, the bottom he
of her full skirt dragging along the dusty floor, "there's a rhyme I reci
to remind myself not to allow my attention to be reflected off th
façade of a thing. A very simple mantra, of sorts, which I will no
teach to you."

The classroom was silent, waiting.

"Cold Fire," she said and smiled at the class. "Dark Bone. Black Mist."

The class repeated after her: *Cold Fire; Dark Bone; Black Mist.*

She was pleased. "Look for the turn, the trick, the twist."

Again, the class repeated after her. *Cold Fire; Dark Bone; Black Mis
Look for the turn, the trick, the twist.*

. . .

When the directress asked me to stay after class, my stomach flipped. What did she know? I swallowed hard and made my way to the front of the classroom while the rest of the scholars shuffled out, whispering amongst themselves and staring at my flattering new hairstyle. I fidgeted, waiting for the last of them to leave before the directress closed the door and offered me a seat. Her silver-white braids were clipped back with metallic clasps, and her eyes were diamond chips.

"Ms. Knight." Her enunciation was as elegant as always.

I cleared my throat, fidgeted in my seat, then gave her my full attention. My anxiety level soared, but I tried to keep my breathing even.

"Your house mistress, Ms.Hook, told me what happened this morning."

Oh, faex, I thought.

"But I'd like to hear your side of the story."

Nervously, I drummed my fingers on my knees.

"She forgot to mention your new hairstyle," said the directress.

I rubbed my scalp self-consciously. "I'm assuming that's what started the trouble. Was it Isadora Crowe who cut your hair off?"

I hesitated. "I was asleep."

I hated Izzy, but I wasn't a snitch. The Ferals had taught me that.

Directress Copperfield didn't look surprised. "Oh," she said, playing along. "I guessed that it was perhaps Ms. Crowe who cut off your hair, and when you woke up, you went to confront her about it."

I sat dead still, not wanting to give anything away.

"And, when you confronted her, you also happened to find the super-glue that she had used last week in your toothpaste."

I continued to look at the woman, feeling intensely uncomfortable.

"I thought that was a nice touch," she said, a hint of amusement on her face. "Perhaps you'll be a detective one day."

I doubted it. I had only one ambition for my future, and that was to kill vampires and avenge my parents' deaths. But no-one pays you to slay vampires, and I'm not one of those trust-fund kid wizards, so I thought that perhaps I should consider it. I could always slay vamps in my spare time. An eccentric hobby, I realised, but no-one's perfect.

"Every city needs a good wizard detective," said Copperfield.

"I'm a girl, though," I said. Yet another reason I didn't fit in; I was the only female wizard in the whole school. All the paranormal detectives I had ever read about were men.

"Somehow, I don't think that will be a problem," she said. "I think we both know that you've got a bright mind and you're a potent spell-slinger. You have a unique magical skill set, and a natural ability we don't often see in this school."

She meant the darkness. The pain. The lucky curse of grief that augments my power.

"It won't be easy," she said, "but nothing in life worth doing is."

Directress Copperfield announced that I was not to blame for the morning's incident, and cancelled my detention so that I'd be able to participate in the archery championship. I was sure I had Ferra to thank for that. The directress did, however, tell me to repair the stall door I had defaced, which made my cheeks blush to burning. I agreed —a little reluctantly—because my repairing magic spell was beyond bad, and I was worried about what further damage I would do.

Despite the promising cool temperature of the morning, the afternoon sun beat down on us as we gathered outside the Astrodome. The students and teachers were already seated inside, and I could hear the excited buzz of the crowd; a giant hive of bees. My nerves began to fray. I was never one for crowds, and I certainly wasn't one for performing in front of people, especially when it was the top three magical schools in South Africa. I clutched my new crossbow, my fingers slippery with sweat. *How did I get here?* I wondered, as an official led us into the humming arena.

Only the top four archers from each school would compete, and I, along with three Copperfield students, had been selected from the school team. We smiled and nodded at each other as we stood in our identical outfits: copper-coloured uniforms embroidered with our school emblem. A few of the kids from the competing schools—dressed in maroon and emerald green—eyed my crossbow with suspicion. Theirs were top of the range and manufactured by well-known companies, and mine, although sleek, was clearly an improvised weapon. I didn't blame them for being suspicious. Anything can happen when magic is involved.

Seeking courage, I looked around for a friendly face in the crowd of spectators but came up blank. Ferra, being the Head Matron, would be slaving away in the kitchen, chopping and tasting and giving orders to the staff, probably simultaneously. The dwarf had always been good at multi-tasking. When I searched the cheering masses, all I saw was a sea of expectant faces. The schools began their war-cries, and the stadium was taken by a Mexican Wave of roaring children as each school had their chance. Ranorth Academy of Sorcery, the green school, went first, followed by the maroon students—Westarth, School of the Arcane. When it was Copperfield's turn, they shook their gold and bronze banners and pom-poms and shouted the words to the school's favourite magical war cry, which made my blood rush, and white noise filled my ears.

· · ·

I knew the drill. I had attended the championship the previous year, held at a competing school, and had fallen in love with the idea of archery. I thought that if my destiny was going to be to kill vampires, best I start practising. I asked the coach if I could join the team. She gave me a second-hand crossbow and the rest is history. So, there I stood, one of twelve, ready to win the prized title.

Rusty, a bronze-pelted werewolf, was moonlighting as the announcer. Usually, he was the guard at the entrance to the school, but today we had a private security team of orcs doing that. Rusty stood at the podium wearing his characteristic lupine scowl, looking handsome in his human form. With his dark lips turned up at the corners, he asked the hyped-up crowd for silence so that we could begin.

The referee was an old wizard I didn't recognise, wearing a planet-spangled cloak and holding an ebony staff. He walked to the centre of the arena and banged his staff on the ground three times, for silence, and the buzz died down. My heart was doing the tango, and I was sure the tall Westarth boy standing next to me could hear it. We took our places, all lined up at the South end of the stadium, facing the field. The crowd sat to the left of us, and the officials to the right.

There were to be three initial rounds, *Volas; Contendis,* and *Ventum.* The final round would be a little more complicated, and the only one in which we were allowed to use magic.

"Round one," announced Rusty. The accompanying teachers of the schools strode in front of the crowds of students and lifted their wands and staffs.

"*Clipeum salutem speculo,*" they said, and a huge screen of safety glass went up between the contestants and the audience. It was high enough to protect them from stray arrows but not too high that they wouldn't be able to hear Rusty.

"Archers, are you ready?" asked the wizard.

Ve all nodded and readied our weapons. I had to wipe the sweat off
ıy hands so that my new crossbow wouldn't slip in my shaking
ngers. One of the officials laid a large basket of apples in the middle
f the arena: poison green, blood maroon, and shining copper—thirty
pples, worth ten points each.

Volus," shouted the old wizard, lifting his staff. The apples rose, and
e aimed. A maroon apple was shot through first, with a sleek bolt
om the Westarth boy next to me. Rusty hurried to add ten points to
ieir score. A green apple fell next, and Rusty adjusted the score. I
ɔok aim at one of the floating copper apples in the distance and
ulled the trigger. The crossbow made a beautiful zinging sound as
ıe bolt rushed down the flight path and speared my apple right in the
ıiddle of its core. Without lowering my bow, I shot three more, and
ne of my fellow Copperfield contestants shot down two. Red and
reen apples fell, too, but I had stopped counting, only focusing on
ringing down the rest of my targets. I missed one, then got it on the
cond try. I heard Rusty announce that Ranorth was in the lead, then
Jopperfield, then Ranorth overtook us again. When Westarth caught
p and kept the winning position, the audience went wild. I took a
allow breath, steadied my arms, and shot down the last four copper
pples in quick succession.

Jne hundred points to Copperfield!" shouted Rusty into his micro-
hone. The rest of the apples fell to the ground, and we lowered our
ows. We were leading by twenty points. The officials retrieved the
ftover apples and lobbed them over the glass shield. Students caught
iem and cheered. A fresh basket of apples was brought out for the
cond round.

'hree contestants, one from each school who had shot down the least
pples, left the playing field and walked around to join the crowd. A
isappointed girl, wearing glasses, got her hair ruffled by her coach. It
emed to cheer her up a bit.

We prepared for the next round, shaking out our arms and finger
then loaded our crossbows and lifted them, ready to let our arrows fly

"*Contendis!*" shouted the wizard, moving his staff around. The thirt
apples flew up into the air, but this time they moved and bounce
around, like nervous lottery balls.

We began shooting, but the things were so easy to miss. I trained m
eyes on the one closest to me and pulled the trigger. The shinin
metallic apple exploded as my bolt struck it, spattering the groun
with apple juice. A green apple was taken down, then another. Th
other Copperfield archers managed three between them, but n
before the Westarth kids got five. I reeled my mind in and focused.
needed to win. With a kind of laser focus I never knew was possible,
shot down six apples in a row. I knew the last one I hit was number te
because they all stopped quivering and dropped. The Copperfiel
students cheered, shook their banners, and threw their pom-poms int
the air.

"Two hundred points to Copperfield!" shouted Rusty, who wa
panting a bit now. The leftover apples were again given to the crow
who got so excited you'd swear they had never seen food in their live
The students with the least hits stepped back and joined the rest c
the spectators. There were six of us left. The scoreboard read Coppe
field 200 / Ranorth 160 / Westarth 150.

The last basket of apples was brought out.

"Archers ready?" asked the old wizard.

We all nodded and brought our crossbows up to our eyes. As
raised mine, I caught a glimpse of someone in the crowd, in the vis
tor's area where the clothes were mostly monochrome instead c
green, red and gold. He was staring at me with an intense look i
his eyes. He was slightly older than me, blond, pale, with shar
cheekbones, and dressed in black. I had a feeling deep in m
stomach that I had met him before, but where? He wasn't Coppe

field alumni, and with a face and posture like that, he was definitely not a Feral.

Before I had even heard the old wizard say *"Ventum"*, my competitors began firing away. I broke eye contact with the blonde boy and grappled with my crossbow, trying to steady my hands and visualise a shot. In the third round, the apples were flung around in a whirlwind. Two green ones were struck, and then a red. I missed three times before I finally got one. Westarth cheered—it had been a maroon one. I had just scored an own-goal. My cheeks flared. The blond boy was still staring at me; eyes like hot coals. I knew then why I recognised him.

He wasn't a Feral, but I had first seen him when I was living on the streets. One night was so bitterly cold, the blond boy put a blanket around me. A year or so later the same boy passed me a takeaway container of food when I was so hungry I thought I might faint in the parking lot outside a discount liquor store. Another red apple went down, and two green. We had lost our lead and were in danger of finishing last. I dragged my eyes away from the boy and tried to hit an apple, but every one of my bolts missed. Irritated with myself, I quickly reloaded and tried again. I hit only one copper apple before the tall Westarth boy next to me exploded their tenth. He pumped his fist in the air.

"And Westarth is now in the lead!" yelled Rusty. The scoreboard read:

Westarth 250 / Renmarth 240 / Copperfield 210.

Deodamnatus, I swore under my breath. I knew I could do better. Disappointment clawed at my insides.

There were three of us left for the fourth and final round, the one that decided the winner. It was a little different. There were no more floating or flying apples; the children's games were over. In the last round, we had chimera to kill.

It sounds extreme, but they were just conjured creatures, illusions we were to strike down for fifty points each. Once you landed your own chimera, you were allowed to take aim at the surviving ones, and earn twenty-five points a pop. We were so behind; I knew I needed to get all three phantoms if I wanted the prize. I refused to look in the direction of the blond boy on the stands, but I knew he was still there; could feel his gaze on me. I took a deep breath and gave myself a quick inner-monologue pep talk.

You've got this.

You've been practising every day for a year.

This is your calling.

Make Ferra proud.

The old wizard stepped forward and lifted his black staff. He muttered his incantation, and I saw the veins pulsing in his neck. *"Evoco et excito, nunc et semper, res ac mortales."*

It was the classic conjuring spell, but I didn't get to hear the details because the onlookers were stamping their feet and going haywire. The wizard raised his arms, and his irises pulsed with an icy blue. Out of his staff billowed three shadow forms which flew up to the top of the Astrodome and began screaming, like demons let out of hell. The noise was ear-splitting, and my instinct was to drop my crossbow and cover my ears, but I held on and raised it, instead, ready to fire my first bolt.

The smoky shadows turned into the three Furies, one scaled with copper, one with shimmering sea-green, one with liquid maroon. I knew about Erinyes—we had studied them in school—but nothing prepared me for how they looked. They were huge demonic women with bat wings and bleeding eyes. On top of their heads were nests of golden vipers. Furies were the three infernal goddesses of vengeance, and they took one look at us and hissed in our faces with breath so sour it brought saliva gushing into my mouth.

Holy Faex!

When I was younger, I used to imagine the Afterlife to be like a kind of Halloween-themed heaven, with ankle-biters dressed as ghouls, and plenty to eat and drink, but looking at these Furies made me understand that hell was real.

The noise of the crowd short-circuited my brain. I had never experienced a chimera before. The Council frowned upon conjuring them up as an unnecessary danger. The witch or wizard who magicked them into being had to have years of experience and a pure heart. They also had to know how to rein them in, because chimeras were notorious for breaking the chains of illusion and taking on a life of their own. The three creatures' multicoloured smoke billowed at us, making us cough and our eyes water. Because of their size, they seemed easier to hit than a small spinning apple, but most of their bodies were made of smoke.

Alecto was the red one, the embodiment of constant anger. Megaera was the green one, driven by jealousy. Tisiphone—the copper chimera I was to kill—was the avenger of murder. I felt it was unfair to have to shoot an avenger. After all, my destiny was to find the vampire who killed my parents and drive an arrow through his heart. We were on the same side, weren't we? But then Tisiphone snarled and rushed at me and tried to take me out with her brass-studded whip. These creatures were no saviours. Their job was to torture souls in the Afterlife, and they wouldn't be able to tell the difference between a friend and an enemy. Their entire countenance was fire and brimstone. Megaera went for the archer in the green uniform and, with a bright snapping sound, took the girl's legs out from under her with her whip. The crowd gasped.

Um. That wasn't supposed to happen. The chimeras weren't supposed to be able to hurt us. I glanced at the old wizard, and my body went cold with shock. He was lying on the floor and jerking as if he were having a seizure.

Filius canis!

Tisiphone barrelled in my direction, and I screamed. I couldn't help it. I clutched at my crossbow, almost dropping it in fright, then recovered. To sharpen my focus, I imagined that the copper-corseted winged Fury was my mother's killer—a giant, evil vampire who had orphaned me; who had almost broken me. My antique wand warmed against my hip. I shot her in the chest, hoping that's where her heart was—if she had one. The bolt travelled straight through her, and she snarled and breathed on me like an angry dragon, flapping her leathery black wings. Alecto flew up to us, too—the horrified audience shrieking and banging on the glass shield—and grabbed the Westarth boy next me. She wanted to take him to the Underworld, perhaps as a new toy. I screamed again as Tisiphone launched herself at me and my trigger finger automatically fired, hitting her in the eye. She shrieked and fell a few feet, but was not deterred. I saw adults gather with their wands out, but they looked tiny and powerless compared the tremendous demon roaring and flapping above me. Megaera, seemingly happy to have knocked the green archer unconscious by flattening her with her whip, took to the shouting crowds. The teachers and officials slung spells to make the glass shield grow taller, shooting up to the ceiling so the demon couldn't hurt any more students. They began to evacuate them, but the Astrodome was ancient and only had one emergency exit. Next thing I knew, Megaera smashed the safety glass, shattering it and sending waves of cobwebbed-glass and shards all over the panicking students.

I remembered my heartache, my never-ending anger, and sense of loss —the difficulty of never belonging. I felt my power rising. Pain, fear, grief ... it all swirled inside me, and I could feel potent magic spreading all the way through my body, from my stomach to my fingertips. I

ened my heart to the assault of emotions and whipped up the spell
ntil it felt like I was about to explode. This was it; this was my
perpower.

ly name is Jacquelyn Denna Knight, and I turn my pain into magic.

ly power rose inside me, a cobalt-coloured smoke sparking with gold.
n intense rush of magic nearly overtook me, but I gathered myself in
me. With everyone else panicking, a strange calm fell over me, like a
ent bubble. Time slowed, the noise faded, the fright fell away. It was
ist me, Tisiphone, and my new weapon. I aimed it at the copper-
aled Fury again, and this time when I released the bolt, I spoke
nfidently. "*Glaciem exquiris.*"

he bolt zinged from my bow, turning to a spear of ice as my spell took
fect. It hit Tisiphone in the chest, and she raised her hands to her
mples and shrieked in anger and pain as she, and the smoke she had
rought along, disappeared.

old Fire, Directress Copperfield had said.

hese demons were from the pits of hell, so ordinary arrows and
ames could not hurt them. They loved fire and were drawn to it. The
emental shock of an icicle in the heart, however, seemed to do the
ick. I aimed my crossbow at the green coloured Fury—Megaera—the
ne who had whipped the Ranorth girl and was now terrorising the
ampeding crowd. She charged at a group of girls, and I saw Izzy
rowe cowering there, about to get snatched up by the vicious
eature.

Vithout hesitating, I sent a frozen bolt at the demon. It struck her in
er head. The scalp-snakes hissed, and Megaera writhed in agony
efore dissipating. Two of the officials dragged the old wizard away
om the arena ground. I wasn't worried anymore. I had taken out two
f the Furies, and I was ready for my trifecta. Alecto looked at me,
apping in the smoky air, still holding the unconscious Westarth boy
her claws. She was high up, and I realised if I killed her, she'd drop

the boy. It was a Mexican standoff—if Mexican standoffs apply t
impromptu battles between girl wizards and hellfire Furies.

I needed some of my Feral magic, my quick and dirty spell-slinging. ·
trick. I needed a distraction, like in the old days when I'd force
breeze to blow a stranger's hat off, then run to get it for him. I'd ste;
his wallet with one hand as I handed over the errant hat with th
other, and be rewarded with a pat on the head. The demon w;
expecting elemental magic, an icy javelin in her ribs.

Cold Fire; Dark Bone; Black Mist. Look for the turn, the trick, the twist

"*Ignem exquiris*," I said, and a comet of fire shot out of my hand
lighting up the ground between us.

I threw my beautiful new crossbow into the flames and raised m
hands in surrender as we watched it burn. Mesmerised, the frant
batting of Alecto's wings slowed. Feeling safer now that I w;
unarmed, she dropped to look at the fire. Once she was low enough t
see the flames reflected in her bleeding eyes, I grabbed my pulsatir
wand from my hip.

I gathered the magic in my chest, ready to let it rip.

"*Glacieum exquiris!*" I shouted, and my wand blasted her with
meteor shower of ice and snow. It hit her so hard she was flung bac
and she dropped the boy. He landed with a thud, but he was movin;
He was alive. I raced over, through what was left of the flames, an
pointed my wand at the demon's splayed form. She was trying to g·
up, but I wasn't going to let her.

"*Nebulum!*" I yelled, and the body of the demon turned into swirlir
smoke and sparks, and then faded away.

The danger had passed. Shocked and relieved, I looked up, war;
wand in hand, and the blond boy with the cheekbones smiled at m

and clapped his hands. The students needed no further encourage-
ment to cheer and rush at me, mobbing me while Rusty shouted into
the broken microphone. Ferra appeared, still in her apron, and gave
me one of her rib-crushing hugs. The students jumped up and down,
hugging me, slapping me on the back. Somehow they got hold of the
prize from the podium and passed it down to me. It was a cheesy
trophy of an apple shot through with an arrow, but I loved it. I knew
the feeling of belonging was temporary, but it felt great to be part of
the team, for once. Izzy slipped a bottle into my hand and winked at
me. It was a potion to make my hair grow back overnight. When I
looked again for the strange, familiar blond boy with sharp cheekbones, he was gone.

10

THE SECRET UNDER MY SKIN

B y the time I realised I'd missed a couple of periods and my breasts were tender, it was too late. The black dread bloomed in my stomach, eroding my appetite and my sleep. I thought about killing myself.

If I killed myself, no one would find out what had happened.

If I took my life, I wouldn't have to harbour the parasite growing inside my body. The only thing that stopped me from slitting my wrists was the knowledge that my mom and dad would be prosecuted.

The State didn't take kindly to people committing suicide.

They hadn't yet found a way to punish citizens in the afterlife; instead, relatives and spouses were arrested.

'Saving Sacred Lives!' said the moving 3D billboards. 'The very hairs on your head are numbered.'

It had always sounded like a threat to me.

I felt guilty and dirty in a way I'd never experienced before; eternally tarnished. One day at school, I started crying and couldn't stop. My 11th-grade teacher sent me home, where I lay in my room, the curtains drawn against the vicious sun. I didn't want to see anyone or anything: the posters of banned rock musicians on my walls, the animated photos, the crêpe paper streamers and ribbons tacked to the edges of my mirror. I threw out my favourite childhood teddy bears because even though their cameras and microphones had broken long ago, I felt as if they were watching me. Everything was tainted, and would never be clean again. I couldn't stop the tears, even when my head and stomach ached from weeping. I couldn't help it. It felt like someone had died.

My mom found me like that, a mess of swollen eyes and patchy skin, vibrating with the urge to self-destruct. She insisted I tell her what was wrong, insisted in a way that I knew I would have to, no matter how much I wanted to keep the secret that was boiling my insides. A part of me thought that if no one knew the truth, life could go back to normal and be good again. The thing growing inside me refused to let that happen. When I finally told my mom—that day on my bed—her face contorted in shock, and her hands flew up to cover her nose and mouth; an impulsive prayer to no-one. My body tensed, waiting to be berated.

Some girls might fear being beaten, thrown out of the house, or sent to the State Home for Blessed Mothers, but my parents weren't like that. They had a fierce love for me which never faltered; it was one of the reasons that telling them was so painful. I was their only child, and we were close. I felt like I had ruined our family, ruined my life, ruined everything. Mom cried and held me tight, and we lay on my bed like that for ages, in the dim room.

My poor girl, she sobbed, *my poor girl.* She only ever let go of me to reach for the tissue box. It was a relief to share my pain, and I was finally able to sleep.

. . .

woke up to Mom whispering to Dad on the phone. He was to buy a
regnancy test on his way home from work, but not from our regular
harmacy. He should go to the one on Solomon Street, a gated
ommunity where politicians and priests lived, and there were fewer
tate security cameras. He was to pay in cash, so there'd be no record
f the transaction. If this weren't possible, we'd have to find another
ay to get one.

And we'll need to call Jules," came Mom's urgent whisper. Jules was
friend; a lawyer. I didn't hear the rest of the conversation, because
ie had started running a bath for me.

eased into the warm water, looking down at my flat stomach. Could
iere really be a baby growing in there? The water was cold by the
me Dad got home. I felt paralysed; it was becoming too real, and I
ished again that I could reach for the razor—or the pills, although I
asn't sure there were enough. The cruel irony was that a failed
iicide attempt would be extremely dangerous. There was a gentle
nock on the door, and I told Mom she could come in. She brought me
towel as I stepped out onto the bathmat, and she wrapped it around
ie as if I were a little girl again.

You're shivering," she said. "You stayed in the bath too long."

he passed me the pregnancy test, the handle of which was broken
pen.

Dad took the microchip out," she said.

peed on the strip, and we didn't have to wait long to see the result.

ONGRATULATIONS! The screen said. *You're ten weeks pregnant.*

. . .

The test's smart chip would have sent an alert to the local munic
pality healthcare organisation, which was run by the State's Medic
Aid Program. Ostensibly, it was to make sure that every pregnar
woman would receive the medical and emotional support they neede
to deliver a healthy baby. There was a year of postpartum care, to
with phone calls from robotic nurses telling you when your baby
checkup was due, when it was time for mandatory vaccinations, an
following up on developmental milestones.

Taking Care of Our People, said the State-sponsored posters. *Pregna*
women need support, the street-corner holograms said. *If you kno*
someone who is expecting, please report it to this number.

Mom dressed me in my softest pyjamas and wrapped me up in m
winter robe, then tucked me under a blanket on the couch in th
sitting room. Dad had made me a hot chocolate, and I cried when h
gave it to me. His tenderness was too much to bear.

"Shhh," he whispered into my ear as he hugged me. "Shhh."

"I'm sorry, Dad," I cried.

"Hey," he said, taking the hot mug away from me and setting it on th
side table. He went down on his haunches, took me by the shoulde
and looked into my eyes. "Listen to me. You have nothing to be sor
about."

"I do," I said, "I do."

He hugged me harder and kissed my temple. "We'll find a way to so
this out." He cast a worried look at Mom, who was standing on th
other side of the room with her arms crossed and a tormented look o
her face. He passed the hot chocolate back to me, and they sat with m
all night. It was a vigil for what could have been.

. . .

"What about that pill?" asked Dad. The one on the black market that was more of a rumour than an established fact.

"Impossible to get," said Mom. "And they'll be able to trace it in her blood when she miscarries."

"We can get a doctor," said Dad. He looked around the sitting room, paranoid, perhaps wondering if there were micro-cams hidden in the ceiling.

"They're so deep underground," said Mom, shaking her head. "I wouldn't know where to find a willing doctor."

Since the State had censored the internet, it was almost impossible to get information like that. Messages were scribbled on shreds of paper and passed from hand to hand, but we didn't have the right contacts.

Social media addiction leads to anxiety and depression, said the State Minister of Mental Health. *Over-exposure of online activities causes illness. It's imperative to Protect Our People.*

"We'll go overseas. We'll go to Sweden. Or Switzerland."

But we all knew that wouldn't work. They pricked your finger before allowing you to check in on any flight and ran it for over a thousand medical conditions, including pregnancy. Pregnant women weren't allowed on aeroplanes anymore. The State coddled civilians to the point of suffocation. *A percentage of pregnant women go into labour while flying,* the digital pamphlets said. *Why Take the Risk?*

Abortion was punishable by death, and back-alley abortions usually resulted in the same sentence but implicated more people. The foetus was the size of a beetle, but I was forced to incubate it or face execution. Watching with horror as my sixteen-year-old body expanded, I'd yearn for the relief and oblivion death would bring, but being executed by the State terrified me. I'd seen people being stoned to death before; fear flared up inside me when I imagined what it would be like. I couldn't do that to myself, or my parents. The electric chair and lethal injection were for less serious crimes—murder and manslaughter—but "baby killers" were seen as the most barbaric. *An Eye for an Eye* said the banners the women in black robes held up. *All Life is Sacred.*

Justice for any crime was swift in the State: the day of arrest to the day of conviction took no longer than a week. Once sentenced to be put to death, the women in black would lead the criminals out onto the stained sandy plain and tie them to the wooden stake buried deep in the ground. They'd ring the bell, and rubbernecking passers-by would stop to watch. A child in the crowd would be encouraged to throw the first stone. All you could hope for was that no loved ones were watching and that the people would kill you quickly.

After weeks of talking and trying to come up with a solution, we understood there was no way out of our predicament. We were forced to report what had happened, and the pregnancy that had resulted from it. When I reached the end of my first trimester, we were notified that the father of the child had been released from prison—a penal labour camp—a year early, for good behaviour, and was to be awarded joint custody rights. It was too much for me. I fled to the bathroom, ready to swallow every pill in the medicine cabinet, but my mom pulled me away. A panic attack roared inside me, and I hyperventilated and collapsed into her arms. I wanted to die, but not even that option was available to me; I could not access even the most basic of freedoms. *Saving Sacred Lives!*

The child's father would be allowed in the birthing room, said the report from the court. He'd be able to hold the baby and snip the umbilical cord. We were to divide our time with the child in a "fair fashion".

Just thinking of him made me feel sick, and desperate with dread. I wanted to vomit violently to expel everything inside me. I retched and retched, but nothing came out. I had flashbacks of the night it happened: the passionate kisses we shared, the warm beer breath on my neck, the skirt I was wearing. The court had made it sound like he had no choice but to tear my panties after I had said no; no choice but to cover my mouth so hard I couldn't breathe. He had been my boyfriend, after all. We had been drinking, after all. *He had a bright future before him,* said the trio of judges. *It wouldn't be right to take that all away from him because of an isolated incident.* It was decided that the blood on my torn underwear wasn't there because he had forced himself on me, but rather because I had been a virgin at the time. *It was unfortunate,* said the judges, *but perhaps we'd be able to patch things up and do the right thing for the baby.*

It was that moment—hearing that my rapist would be in the birthing room and my life forever after—which made up my mind. I refused to be their flesh-and-blood incubator. Let them stone me to death.

∽

11

A TREE IN A FOREST

The married couple, Eddie and Roberta, had to drag the old man into the plush reception of the EverAfter frail care centre.

"Pops!" beseeched Eddie. He was sweating with the effort. "Don't fight us, please!"

"We love you, Pops," said Roberta, her eyes shining with tears. "We're bringing you here because we love you. Because it's the best place for you to be." Her jewellery flashed under the artificial lights.

"They can take care of you here, Pops," said Eddie.

"Don't call me that!" shouted the old man, trying to wrench his elbow away from Eddie. "I'm not your father!"

The smartly dressed receptionist left his station and came around the white marble counter, a concerned look on his face. He clicked a button on his silver headset; a modern Madonna halo.

"We need two orderlies at reception," he said into the speaker.

The old man managed to break away from Roberta and kick over a metal tray nearby, the contents of which went clattering all over the floor, along with Eddie's Rolex.

"Make that *four* orderlies, and a gurney," said the male Madonna, then switched the headset off. He scooped the watch off the floor. "You're the Malones, I assume?"

Eddie and Roberta looked up at him at the same time. "Yes," said Roberta. "We called ahead."

"Let go!" Pops roared. He was tall, and stooped, and looked a hundred years old—and that was being kind. His hair floated in an untidy cloud around his head, his skin was as mottled as an octopus's, and his teeth were the colour of illegal ivory.

"Yes," said Madonna, passing the Rolex back to Eddie. "We've been expecting you. Mr. Malone's room is ready."

"Phone my son!" shouted the old man. "Phone my son, and he'll tell you that I don't know these people and that I don't belong here!"

Eddie looked distraught. "I *am* your son, Pops."

"You're a liar!" yelled the ancient man, stabbing his dead branch of finger into Eddie's chest. His clothes were old and tattered, and every time he moved, he emanated a wave of sickly body odour. Not just body odour, but Old Person Body Odour. The couple was used to it, but the receptionist's nostrils flared. He gave the couple a sympathetic—if not shallow—smile. There was a reason he worked at the front desk, instead of as a nurse, or an orderly.

As if on his mental cue, four well-built men appeared.

"Thank you," Roberta said, finally able to let go of the old man and put her hand on her chest as a gesture of relief. The rings on her fingers sparkled as she fixed her hair. She turned to the receptionist. "His favourite dinner is spaghetti Bolognese, and he likes to watch golf."

"I hate watching golf!" shouted the old man. "It's as boring as hell!"

"He likes his tea really hot, and strong," said Roberta. "Milk. One sugar. And he must have his dinner at seven on the dot, or he begins to get anxious."

Eddie piped up. "He needs his sleeping pills at nine, or he'll be up all night."

"I've never taken a sleeping pill in my life!" yelled Pops. "I don't even know who these people are!"

"It's all on the admission form we filled in," said Eddie. "It's all there."

Roberta watched the orderlies with an appalled expression as they restrained the old man.

"He'll be okay here, with us," said Madonna. "It's an excellent facility."

"We know," nodded Roberta. "We know. We did our homework. We don't want to abandon him ... we just want the best for him. His state of mind—"

"I don't know what your plan is—" said Pops.

"You're breaking our hearts!" cried Roberta. "Can't you see how much this is hurting Eddie?" There were tears in her eyes, and when she blinked, they escaped and ran down her cheeks. Eddie looked suitably hurt.

The orderlies struggled with the old man, who was still fighting tooth and yellowed nail.

"Be gentle with him!" shouted Eddie. "For God's sake, he's *frail!*"

"I'll give you frail!" yelled Pops, who lunged for one of the orderlies with a knotted fist. The men in white uniforms increased their force.

"You're going to injure him!" yelled Roberta.

"Londiwe," said Madonna, and one of the orderlies looked up. The receptionist gave him a signal, and Londiwe stepped away and pulled an injector pen out of his utility belt. He moved towards Pops and darted the old man in the thigh with the tranquilliser. At first, the couple thought it hadn't worked, because Pops was still trying to land punches, but suddenly he stopped, swayed, and fell like a tree in the forest. The muscled men caught him before he hit the tiled floor. They heaved him onto the gurney and strapped his wrists and ankles with black velcro.

"Take him to his room, for now," instructed the receptionist. "We'll guide him through orientation later when he's feeling better."

"We'll go with him," said Roberta, moving towards the stretcher. "I don't want him waking up all alone in a strange room."

"With all due respect," said Madonna, "it's probably best if you don't."

"But he's my father!" said Eddie.

"Mr. Malone," said the receptionist. "I understand that this is a very trying time for you. But at this stage of dementia, it's best for all parties involved to avoid traumatic situations. Your father is clearly upset by your presence—it's not unusual at all—so let's keep the contact at a minimum, for now."

"I'm afraid he'll fight the nurses and get hurt," Roberta blurted.

"No. That won't happen. We'll keep your father sedated for as long as it takes him to settle in. The hardest part is over."

Roberta nodded, wiping the smudged mascara from beneath her eyes.

"Thank you," said Eddie.

Unconscious and secured to the gurney, they covered Pops with a heavy blanket. Eddie hugged his limp body; Roberta squeezed his cold claw of a hand. The old man's mouth gaped open in a silent snore.

"Goodbye, Pops," they said. "We love you."

The receptionist gave the signal, and Eddie and Roberta held hands as they watched the orderlies wheel Pops away.

Eddie and Roberta put their sunglasses on as they left the building, and climbed into their black Mercedes. As they drove out of the Ever-After frail care centre's parking lot, Roberta pulled off her wig, leaned back on the headrest, and sighed. "That was a tough one."

"It was," agreed Eddie. "I didn't expect him to be such a fighter."

"He's much stronger than he looked on his file."

"You were great, though," said Eddie, squeezing Roberta's knee. He put on a high-pitched voice and did his best impression of his wife. "*His favourite dinner is spaghetti Bolognese, and he likes to watch golf.*"

Roberta chuckled. "Next time, I'll change it up, so we don't get bored."

"Either way, you looked great as a red-head. And you deserve an Oscar. Who's next on the list?"

Roberta opened the glove compartment and took out a piece of paper and a pen. She used the back of the pen to scratch her scalp, which was itchy from wearing the wig. At the top of the paper in her hands was the logo for a local dementia support group. She crossed off number fourteen: Miles "Pops" Malone.

"The next one is a woman," she said. "In Killarney. Alice Germaine."

"Are you ready to be Alice Germaine's distraught daughter?" asked Eddie.

"Of course I am," said Roberta, fluttering her eyelashes. "Are you ready to be her hand-wringing son-in-law?

"You know me," said Eddie, adjusting his seat to get more comfortable for the journey. "I'm pretty good at hand-wringing."

Roberta looked thoughtful for a moment. "I think we'll go for quiche and Hallmark movies for Mom."

"Yes. Quiche and Hallmark movies," said Eddie, turning a corner. He squinted into the sun. "What kind of quiche?"

"Ham and mushroom? With cheese."

"Perfect." He rounded another corner, heading out of the suburb. "How are we doing on the business side of it?"

"I borrowed her daughter's identity with the data you hacked, and the bank accepted the medical history file and the power of attorney letter. The transfer of Alice Germaine's funds into our account has been initiated. It couldn't have been easier."

"Excellent."

"The Twelve Oaks Retirement Village in Illovo is expecting her to arrive this time next week, so I hope it'll be transferred before then."

"Shouldn't be a problem," said Eddie, as he accelerated along the ramp to get onto the highway. "It'll be good to get Mom into a place where they can care for her properly."

"Yes." Roberta nodded sagely. "It will be the best place for her to be."

~

12

NACHTHEXEN

I t wasn't about revenge; it was about love, and justice.

When I heard about what Mariya Oktyabrskaya did, I realised what was required of me. We had the same first name and the ime passion for killing the fascist pigdogs that were invading our eloved Motherland and killing our people. I was only 23, but my estiny was clear.

had never met Oktyabrskaya, but I knew all about her. She was a eroine, a *zavodila*, and her mission was tattooed on my heart. We had atched from separate towns during Operation Barbarossa as millions f German troops streamed over our borders and gunned down omen and children who were fleeing the attack. We saw young boys ot, mothers cut down, babies slaughtered.

lariya and I had travelled a similar road. I thought of her as my *oputchik*: a stranger who becomes a companion while you travel in ne same direction. That night, after the first brutal invasion, a pristine yer of snow had fallen, covering the corpses we had not yet been able move. White and stiff, they looked like toppled statues. I cried for weeks and could not get out of bed; my mind felt broken. The world felt broken.

When Mariya Oktyabrskaya heard her husband had been killed in battle, she sold her home and all her possessions. She sent the money to the Red Army and asked Stalin if she could have an army tank. A few months later, Mariya was a trained mechanic and tank driver. Her T-34 had the name "Fighting Girlfriend" emblazoned on the side, as per her request. In a time when few women knew how to drive cars Oktyabrskaya rode her tank to the front line where she mercilessly mowed down the enemy, earning the respect of her fellow soldiers.

When I thought of how Hitler had breached the peace pact I wished I could strangle the man. When I thought of my dead friends and family lying in the streets, their blood running in the gutters, I got so angry that I couldn't breathe. But when I thought of my *poputchik,* I felt emboldened and strong. I believed I could make a difference, even if it meant I would burn.

I didn't know much about the Night Witches, but I had heard rumours. The motherland celebrated the aviatrixes for their bravery and determination. They wrought havoc with the Nazi war machine from the Caucasus Mountains to the outskirts of Berlin; they were loved in Russia and feared in Germany. Nazis suspected there was sorcery involved, saying the female pilots flew planes that sounded like witches' brooms and had night vision, like cats. The *Nachthexen* were so fearsome to the Germans that any member of the Luftwaffe who managed to shoot down one of their planes would automatically get awarded an Iron Cross.

I wrote to Raskova, applying to enlist in the all-female night bomber regiment she had formed. Raskova was also a *zavodila;* she inspired people through her courage and grit. I couldn't afford a tank, but I had excellent eyesight and good instinct, and a hunger to see the Nazis burn.

When Raskova accepted me for training, my belief in my destiny was confirmed. I packed a small leather case and the well-thumbed photograph I had of Vladik, my fiancé, and I made my way to Engels. He was the only living person left in my life who I loved, and who loved me. But he was away, fighting the Nazis, so I had nothing to keep me in my hometown except bleak memories and heartbreak. In Russian, there is a word that describes a deep longing, intense anguish, an ache of the soul. No word in English renders all the shades of *toska,* but when I thought of the simple, happy life I used to lead, and how much I worried about Vladik, I was overcome with it.

On my arrival, my hair was cropped short, and I was given an oversized man's uniform to wear. I punctured a new hole in the belt with a sharp screwdriver from the workshop and wrapped the leather tightly around my waist, so it didn't look too bad, and tucked the photograph of Vladik into my breast pocket. Some of the other pilots used their navigation pencils to colour their lips, but I didn't care too much about that. There'd be plenty of time for pretty things once we had defeated the pigdogs. I would wear dresses again, and makeup, and lie in Vladik's arms all day. But *dacha* would only happen once the war was over and Mother Russia was ours again.

I didn't mind the masculine uniforms or unflattering hairstyle. I didn't care about the uncomfortable bed or bland food, or the way we'd have to wash in cold water when there was no fuel available to heat it. What did shock me was seeing the squadron's planes for the first time.

I didn't know anything about aviation, but even a fool could see the planes were nothing but old, obsolete crop-dusters.

"Are you joking?" I said to Kirochka, a broad-shouldered woman whose job it was to induct the new trainees. She called me *pochemuchka* because I asked so many questions.

She laughed and slapped her hands on her generous hips. "Not joking," she replied, and then her smile disappeared. They were Polikarpov Po-2 biplanes, made of old plywood and canvas, and never meant for combat. They had neither radios nor radars, yet they were only ever flown at night.

"Don't get hit by a tracer bullet," said Kirochka, her face now solemn. I assumed it would result in the whole aircraft igniting like the paper planes they resembled. Some were decorated with flowers, and I couldn't help thinking that although it looked pretty, they reminded me of cheap caskets.

The biplanes had many drawbacks. Because they were so light, they could only carry the weight of two bombs, which meant that the pilots had to fly back to reload at least a dozen times during the night raids, sometimes as many as eighteen. It also meant there was no space for guns or parachutes. Seeing the planes made me nervous, but I kept reminding myself that these women were going out night after night on successful missions and coming back alive. If they could do it, so could I. Kirochka squeezed my shoulder as she related the benefits of the small planes. While it was true that a mere bullet could cause you to explode in mid-air and give the pigdogs a fancy pyrotechnic show while you plummeted to the ground like a hell comet, there were also numerous benefits to having such a small, flimsy aircraft.

"Size isn't everything," she said, winking at me.

It turned out that the crop-dusters were too small to be detected by the enemy's radars, and the sluggish flying speed afforded them more agility than the German fighter planes. Their strategy of cutting their engines as they approached the target meant the aviatrixes could approach in silence, under the cover of darkness, and deliver their payload without being detected. Their invisibility and silence was a deadly combination. By the time I joined the 588th night bomber regiment they had already undertaken 24,000 missions and dropped 16,000 tons of bombs on German targets. They were helping to turn the tide of World War II.

Two months after I began training, Kirochka arrived in the workshop while I was elbow-deep in grease, working on a stalled engine.

"Go to your dorm. Get some rest. You'll be going on your first raid tonight."

My mouth became instantly dry, and the photograph of Vladik seemed to burn in my pocket.

"Tonight?" I asked. I hadn't been there as long as some other young women.

"You're ready," she said.

I didn't feel ready, but the more the picture in my breast pocket burned, the braver I got. I was there to stop the war and spare Vladik's life. I was there for the fight, so best I began fighting.

I lay on the rough grey blanket on my bunk, but there was no chance of sleep as my stomach cramped with fear. When I heard Sebrova's call to rally for the evening's briefing, I started sweating and wanted to tell Kirochka that I had decided I wasn't ready.

I knew what she would say.

You'll never feel ready, Mariya. No one ever feels ready to fly, sightless, into the night sky. Avos'.

Avos' is the ingrained Russian concept of blind trust in sheer luck.

Think about your home town.

Blood running red in the gutters. Powder snow. Fallen statues.

Think of your beloved fiancé, she'd say. *It's how well you live that makes a difference, not how long.*

I hurried to the toilet and got there just in time to not soil my ill-fitting second-hand uniform.

Who had worn this uniform before? I wondered. *Who had died in it?*

I got to Sebrova's briefing a few minutes late but was not scolded. Kirochka handed me a cup of tea, which I accepted gratefully. A large map was laid out in the centre, with coins marking that night's targets; the kopeks and rubles weighted the map down as the corners flapped in the early evening breeze. The sun was beginning to set, and there was ruby-coloured light on the other aviatrixes' anxious faces.

Sebrova looked at me. "We have a problem."

When it was dark enough to begin, I was trembling all over. I lifted my helmet above my head and pushed it on, tying the clasp tightly beneath my chin. I felt as if I was shaking everywhere, inside and out.

Kirochka must have seen the look of utter dread on my face because she gave me a stern look and said, "Remember why we are doing this, *pochemuchka.*"

She had lost a brother in a Nazi invasion. I nodded at her but didn't trust myself to speak. The photo in my pocket continued to burn. I would save Vlad, and we'd get married and have children. As my late mother used to say, one generation plants the trees, the next gets the shade. It was an old Russian proverb. By fighting against the violent ivasion of our land, I was planting trees for Vladik's and my children, nd our grandchildren.

Ve climbed into the plane, and again I was reminded of how it looked ke a coffin with wings. Kirochka would do the flying, and I was to avigate with my map and compass, as I had been taught. The engine pared to life, and she looked back at me, asking if I was okay. I had no lood left in my face, and I was sure I looked like a ghost. Terrified, I odded. We started rumbling down the strip, and soon the plane lifted ff the ground. It felt as if my stomach had been left behind on the irred gravel. Plunging ahead into the black sky towards the enemy /as a terror rivalled only by the day the Nazis had razed my home. ack then I was powerless, but now I was in a plane carrying two ombs in its belly.

ecause it was an open cockpit, our faces were almost immediately ozen by the rushing wind. I couldn't imagine being that cold for a /hole flight, never mind a dozen of them. It was no wonder some of ie pilots would complain of frostbite stinging their skin. My nerves :ayed further and further the closer we got to enemy territory, like the parkling fuse of dynamite. Before aviation training, I was brave with iy words, calling Nazis *poshlost' pigdogs* and spitting on the ground, ut now my courage had deserted me, and the map shook in my hands.

Ve approached the border. My stomach clenched. Sebrova, the pilot /ho briefed us, had explained how the Germans had just imple- iented rings of powerful searchlights around likely targets. The Jight Witches had always had the advantage of approaching unseen nd unheard, but that was about to change.

Ve flew in a formation of three, piloted by Kirochka, Sebrova, and uliya. Our first target was a bridge crossing, where we saw the readed beams of light searching the ink stain sky. We were so close to ie ground that I knew if we were sighted, they'd incinerate us on the spot. The other two planes—Sebrova's and Yuliya's—hurtled in from of us as we all headed directly toward the roving spotlights. As soo they were sighted, the gunfire began, which was a signal for Sebrov and Yuliya to fly in opposite directions and zig-zag to avoid the bullet While the lights and the guns aimed at the decoys, Kirochka cut ou engine. We stole silently into the dark space just above the target an deployed our bombs. There was a massive explosion on the ground, deafening blast, rumbling and hot. As Kirochka pulled up to avoid th heatwaves and debris, I felt overcome with a breathtaking euphori. Our plan had worked, the crossing was destroyed, and we ha survived. The flight of the Night Witches' broom was the last thin those pigdogs had heard before they were blown to bits, and the bridg was nothing but a dead man's memory.

We used the same strategy six times over until we had delivered a three planes' payloads. I was feeling exhilarated as we headed back t base to reload. Every Nazi we killed, every cold-blooded Germa soldier we stopped by demolishing a road or railway was one le soldier who could hurt Vladik. We flew sixteen successful missior that night, while the picture of my lover in my breast pocket kept m from freezing. I felt the black sky billowing inside my body, and made me feel light, so light that sometimes it felt like I didn't have body at all, that my spirit was flying above the plane.

On the way back to our final landing, I heard Kirochka cry out. M elation vanished as I spotted what had made her exclaim. A dozen c more Luftwaffe planes were heading straight towards us. Three flims gimcrack crop dusters piloted by exhausted women versus a flight c sophisticated Heinkel Eagle-Owl night fighters. Kirochka had to stic her head out from behind the icy windshield to get a clear view c them. The next thing I knew, my spirit shot straight back into my bod as the German pilots blasted us with everything they had. We saile through a wall of enemy fire, and I could feel and smell the bullets as they tore past us. Kirochka dipped, taking advantage of the biplane's agility, and we were able to dodge the deluge of shells that now cracked above us. I was too afraid to peer back at Sebrova and Yuliya, but soon they caught up with us, and we all cheered madly as we readied to land.

By the time I saw the wing was on fire, it was too late. One of the enemy's bullets had clipped it, and the plywood was alight, its flame fed by the rushing air around us. I unclipped my safety harness easily, but taking off my tight leather belt with frozen fingers took forever. I watched the fire hungrily inch up the wing towards us and the fuel tank with a feeling of panic and futility. Finally, I was able to wrench the belt off, and then my jacket. I crawled over to the burning wing, the bitterly cold wind slicing into my body as I left the shelter of the cockpit. I screamed as I almost got blown off. Gripping the wing harder, clutching it with all the strength I had, I tried again to creep towards the fire. This time I reached it and used my jacket to swat the flames. I swore in the dirtiest Russian I knew when the fire refused to die.

I went out further, losing my grip again, and almost tumbling off. I momentarily lost my sanity and imagined the fire was a Nazi creeping toward me. I beat him with my heavy jacket, I hit and punched him, no longer caring if I lived or died. I went berserk, screaming and pounding until the imaginary Nazi fell off the wing, and the fire was out. I dragged my body back into the pit, debilitated and brittle from the biting cold, and pulled my scorched jacket back on. There was no time to celebrate. I had stopped the fire from reaching the fuel tank, but the damage was done. The plane listed sideways and began to drop. *Oh,* I thought, *Kirochka will have to make an emergency landing.* That was okay, we all knew how to do that, and she was one of the best pilots in the squadron. But then I realised that you can't make an emergency landing with one wing. You can't do anything with one wing except crash. I scrambled to put my safety belt on again and pulled my jacket around my body so that I could feel Vladik's face against my breast. Sebrova and Yuliya—who had been flying slowly beside our doomed aircraft—saluted Kirochka, and she returned the gesture. I was glad that I couldn't see the expression on her face.

We crashed just a few miles from our air base. Kirochka's expertise meant we made it as close to base as we could. Her knowledge of the land ensured we found the softest spot to go down, and just as the sun peeked from behind the horizon, we slammed into a golden field of wheat. When I regained consciousness, the sun was slightly higher in the sky, and the breeze made the swaying grain so beautiful I thought I must be in heaven. But as the pain flooded my body I understood I was very much alive. Every bone felt broken, but I was able to move, so I assumed they weren't. When I looked down, my body was bright with blood. I thought I was dying, then saw that it was coming from my nose, which had smashed into the back of Kirochka's seat as we had crashed.

"Kirochka!" I shouted, my voice came out sounding strangled. "Kirochka! We made it!"

My relief energised me enough to climb out of my seat and get to the woman whose intelligence and expertise had saved our lives.

I leaned against her door and took her by the shoulder, as she had so often done to me. When she looked at me, I could see the sunrise and golden fields reflected in her eyes.

"Kirochka!" I was still unable to believe we had survived.

"Look at you," she said. I could see she wanted to laugh but was in too much pain. She made an effort to swallow and then told me to take off my helmet. I didn't understand why, but I obeyed. The helmet was studded with bullets, as was the bloodstained map in my seat. I took a step back; the fuselage was riddled with holes. It was nothing less than a miracle that we were still breathing. I looked in my scorched breast pocket for the photo of Vlad, but it was gone. It must have blown away while I was putting out the fire. There was an immediate sense of loss, but also of joy, because despite all odds, I would live to fight another day, and fight I would. Not only had I survived, but I had been reborn as a real soldier, ready to practise the deadly precision Kirochka had taught me. I would take out a Nazi for every bullet hole in the plane, and every stud in my helmet, and then I'd take out double that, then triple.

The scent of the burnt fabric of my uniform reached me, and I imagined the picture of my beloved floating into the cold and hungry night sky. It was at that moment I tumbled to the realisation that Vladik was dead. How else did I dodge the wall of fire without getting hit by even one bullet? Vladik was dead, and his spirit had enfolded me; protected me.

I was too shocked to sob.

Kirochka made a burbling sound, so I stepped towards her again. I could hear the military vehicle buzzing in the distance, driving in our direction to pick us up and take us back to our base. I looked forward to food and sleep.

Kirochka looked pointedly at the scarred helmet in my hand. "My dear Mariya," she said, smiling at me. "You will live long."

I glanced again at my helmet, then my eyes travelled to her torso, which I saw was bleeding profusely. A sob caught in my throat. My first instinct was to shout *No!* And to put pressure on the wounds to stem the flow, but then I understood the damage was too dire, and that Kirochka was taking what would be her last breaths. I wanted them to be peaceful, not panicked.

Nothing disappears, she used to say to me. *It only changes.*

Mariya Oktyabrskaya, the Fighting Girlfriend.

Vladik.

Kirochka.

These were the sturdy shoulders on which I would stand and do battle.

Kirochka's body collapsed back into her seat. I leaned in and hugged her, thanking her as the flaxen field swayed around us. The sky turned a silvery blue. As she shuddered to stillness, I thought that perhaps she would see her brother again.

DEAR READER

Thank you for supporting my work. I hope you find as much meaning in reading it as I do in writing it!

If you are ready for more, my next collection, Sticky Fingers 5, is available to order.

Perfect for fans of Gillian Flynn and Roald Dahl, these stories are guaranteed to get under your skin.

"Lawrence makes every word count, telling each story with elegance and emotional punch." — Patsy Hennessey

"Each story is masterfully constructed ... Humorous, touching, creepy, but most of all entertaining, this collection is superb." — Tracy Michelle Anderson

Thank you for supporting my work, and happy reading!

Janita

www.jt-lawrence.com